DC

Andrea had been a junior partner in Dr Garth Howard's practice at Ludlow for nearly eighteen months. Their relationship was friendly, but professional—two busy doctors with no time to talk, or get to know each other. Until suddenly all that changed . . .

Sonia Deane is a widow with one son, lives in the Cotswolds, and has written over 120 books. The Doctor-Nurse stories were fortuitous. She chose a doctor hero and from then her readers wanted a medical background. Having personal friends who are doctors enables Sonia Deane's research to be verified. She has also been out with an ambulance team and donned a white coat in hospital!

DOCTOR DECEIVED

BY

SONIA DEANE

MILLS & BOON LIMITED
15–16 BROOK'S MEWS
LONDON W1A 1DR

All the characters in this book have no existence outside the imagination of the Author, and have no relation whatsoever to anyone bearing the same name or names. They are not even distantly inspired by any individual known or unknown to the Author, and all the incidents are pure invention.

The text of this publication or any part thereof may not be reproduced or transmitted in any form or by any means, electronic or mechanical, including photocopying, recording, storage in an information retrieval system, or otherwise, without the written permission of the publisher.

This book is sold subject to the condition that it shall not, by way of trade or otherwise, be lent, resold, hired out or otherwise circulated without the prior consent of the publisher in any form of binding or cover other than that in which it is published and without a similar condition including this condition being imposed on the subsequent purchaser.

First published in Great Britain 1986 by Mills & Boon Limited

© Sonia Deane 1986

Australian copyright 1986 Philippine copyright 1986

ISBN 0 263 75541 X

Set in 10 on 12 pt Linotron Times
03–1086–51,700

Photoset by Rowland Phototypesetting Ltd Bury St Edmunds, Suffolk Made and printed in Great Britain by William Collins Sons & Co. Ltd, Glasgow

CHAPTER ONE

ANDREA heard Garth's voice echoing from the direction of the surgery, and was not prepared for the excitement that mingled with the pleasure of his return. She was twenty-five, and had been a junior partner in his practice in Ludlow for nearly eighteen months. Their relationship was friendly, but professional.

'I'm here,' she called from her desk in her consulting room, her heart quickening its beat as he appeared in the doorway.

'It's good to be back,' he exclaimed heartily, as though he had been in Surrey for a century instead of two weeks on a duty visit to his parents.

'It's good to *have* you back.' She tried to keep her voice steady, but tensed as she became acutely conscious of him. He was, she thought, a striking man with enquiring, disturbing eyes and a dynamic personality. His hair was dark, and shaped to emphasise his fine forehead. She was aware, also—somewhat bemused by her meticulous observations—that he seemed taller, his shoulders broad, hips narrow. Until then he had been Dr Howard, first, and Garth, second. Now, suddenly, that seemed reversed.

'You look startled—surprised,' he said in his deep persuasive voice which could be sharp on occasion.

'I didn't think you'd be back until later.'

They gazed at each other as though their words were totally inadequate. The separation had, in some subtle fashion, changed things. His look was intent, and suggestive of discovery. Garth thought, 'I never realised how beautiful she is,' as he noticed her large, dark grey eyes, flushed cheeks, and hair which the sun turned to gold as it struck from a window behind her.

'I've missed all this.' His sigh was of pleasurable relief. 'I don't belong down there, Andrea. It's a strain—a duty.'

'Ah.' It was an exclamation of understanding. Emotion touched them.

'You and I have never really talked,' he commented, his gaze deepening as it met hers.

She forced a little laugh to avoid seriousness. 'No *time*! Two busy doctors!'

'Or two blind ones,' he added significantly.

The implication of his words shook her, and she hastened on, a little nervously, 'By the way, I've engaged a new nurse. You gave me a free hand and trusted my judgment. Now we shall have Mrs Boyer for the secretarial work, Clare for reception, and we certainly needed someone trained to relieve us of the routine blood-pressure checks, etcetera. Nurse Drake has her SRN, and . . .'

'Fine,' he interrupted. 'We're agreed on that necessity, but I'm in no mood for staff or nurses at the moment. We'll talk shop tomorrow. My holiday doesn't end until midnight!'

Andrea laughed. 'I can take a hint! I'm still on duty.'

'On the contrary—unless having a meal here with me constitutes that,' he suggested unexpectedly.

She looked at him, eyebrows raised. They had never had a meal alone together, either here at his house, Clee View, or at any hotel and restaurant.

'Thank you; I'd like that kind of duty!'

He smiled broadly.

'Edwards and Lily will have prepared a feast.' (Edwards and Lily ran the house for him.) 'I'll go and let them know I'm home and tell them you are joining me.'

'They've been saying, "Nothing seems right without Doctor"!'

Garth's smile was warm and generous. 'I'm singularly fortunate that they grew tired of hotel life and wanted to settle in a permanent job.'

It flashed through Andrea's mind that Garth always talked as though, at thirty-one, his future was settled both domestically and emotionally. While there was nothing of the confirmed bachelor about him, his name had not been linked with any particular woman, although he was exceedingly popular among them, as he was with his colleagues.

When he went from the room, eager and enthusiastic, everything seemed to come to life and the Georgian house, just off Broad Street, took to itself a different personality, the sun pouring in like limelight on a stage. Andrea loved Clee View; its space and elegance was without any element of cold superiority. She locked up the practice quarters. The silence was deep; the waiting room, with its rows of empty chairs, holding the secrets of those who mutely occupied them morning and evening. Fear, expectancy, tragedy, relief, leaving ghosts that lingered with uncanny persistence.

Mrs Boyer's office and a reception area led off ultimately to a common room where Clare—bright, twenty-two and cheerful—produced cups of coffee miraculously in times of stress and still managed to soothe apprehensive patients. Mrs Boyer was always in command, and at forty was smart, sharp and reliable. Andrea hoped Nurse Drake would fit in with the harmonious team . . . It struck her that Garth had not mentioned time for dinner. It was now nearly seven. Should she return to her flat, which was in an old half-timbered converted house near the castle, and change? She had already renewed her lipstick and brushed her hair after surgery ended, although she would not have admitted that the reason was a precaution against Garth returning unexpectedly.

His voice hailed her from the main hall.

'No more paperwork. Come and have a drink. You don't want to go back to the flat? We shall eat around eight.' The words were more a statement than a question.

She looked down at her blue skirt and smoothed her white blouse. 'Only a question of changing,' she admitted.

'You look charming.'

'Thank you.'

They glanced at each other a little hesitantly, as they crossed the hall which was conveniently away from the surgery. It was oak-panelled, and the staircase curved up from a large window to a wide visible landing.

Garth talked as they moved into the sitting room. 'I'm always grateful that my grandfather left me enough money to buy this house,' he said honestly. 'I could never have afforded it.' He added with a whimsical grin, 'And the fact that it was previously owned by a Dr Knowles, who practised here . . .'

'Had you any ties in Shropshire, or Ludlow?' she asked casually, thinking how little she really knew about him.

'None whatever. A mutual friend put me in touch with Dr Knowles. It progressed from there. I wanted to get away from Surrey, where I previously practised; the proximity of Guildford—to the family—was claustrophobic . . . You are fortunate, as I've said before, to have your roots here.' He paused by the drinks tray. They'd seldom had a drink together, and he was not aware of her taste.

'A dry martini, please,' said Andrea in answer to his mute inquiry.

He made it expertly and joined her in the choice. They settled comfortably in their respective chairs. The lofty-ceilinged room was furnished in Regency style, and Persian rugs adorned the parquet flooring. A massive bookcase and corner cupboard gave a friendly atmosphere. In the distance, the Clee Hills were etched against the clear blue sky, and a little walled-in garden (a feature of a few houses in Ludlow) completed a picture of unique charm.

Andrea watched him. She had never seen anyone so relaxed, or in such command of himself, without trace of smugness or conceit.

'This is a lovely room,' she said.

'It's quite absurd that you've been in it so rarely.' His expression was tinged with regret.

She replied, 'Oh, I don't know: people need not live in each other's pockets because they work together. Familiarity can spoil things.'

'There's a happy medium.'

At that, she laughed. 'If there is, then few ever achieve it.' She was wary, not wanting anything to endanger this new excitement.

'Or really want it!' He added wryly, 'Oh, it has all the virtues, admittedly—but, then, so has an egg!'

They laughed together.

'Meaning that without salt . . .' she suggested.

'Exactly.'

'I'm very content with my life,' she insisted, almost on a note of warning.

'Which makes two of us.' His voice was smooth.

The telephone, switched through from surgery, rang, and they groaned in unison. Andrea answered it.

'Stephanie!' she said, her smile dying, as an overwrought voice rushed on, 'Dr Forbes, can I see you tomorrow? Forgive me for troubling you now, but I'm desperate . . . Nothing to do with contraception.' She added in a whisper, 'Mummy mustn't know. She's going to a lunch, so if . . .'

Andrea didn't hesitate. 'Make it one o'clock,' she said with quiet reassurance.

'Oh, thank you!' The line went dead.

'Trouble,' she said gravely as she replaced the receiver.

'Surely not in the Landon family?' Garth looked surprised. 'They have everything: a son, a daughter, unlimited means, beautiful house, swimming pool; garage stocked with cars——' He tried to keep the hint of mockery from his words.

Stephanie's mother, Myrna Landon, was not his type. A fashion-plate, pencil-thin, who always tried to convey the impression that she was on familiar terms with royalty, and that all her friends and acquaintances sat at the top table. Humphrey Landon was an ambitious man who saw his possessions as stepping-stones to social eminence. To his credit, he had started his own business, struggled and fought, and was now owner of a highly successful meat-canning factory. And while his wife's dinner parties were an asset, she could never be said to grace them. The staff worked well for their fair wages, but without trace of devotion. Myrna would never understand that there were times when a friendly handshake told more about a person than diamonds.

'But nothing to do with contraception, apparently.'

He made a significant grunt. 'That makes a welcome change, as things are today. Let's see . . . she's about fifteen?'

'Yes.' Andrea added, 'I'm very fond of her. She's not in the least affected by the artificiality.'

'Whatever's wrong, you'll be able to deal with it.'

'Thank you!' She smiled. 'You must go away more often.'

'I didn't need to go away in order to appreciate your skills.'

And as he spoke, their awareness of each other sharpened. Attraction, sensual and overpowering, flashed between them.

She deliberately changed the mood. 'I would like to talk about Nurse Drake.'

Somewhat to her surprise, he capitulated.

'If you like her and think she is what we've been looking for, I don't see any problems . . .'

'She can start next Monday; trained at St Luke's in London, living in London, of course, during that time. Now she is at The Manor in Cardiff . . . been there a year . . . staff nurse.'

'How old?'

'Thirty.'

'Then, if she's a staff nurse, more than likely to become a Sister. What does she want with a job like this?'

'A change.'

'Which means she'll be off at the drop of a hat!'

'On the contrary, she was most emphatic about that.'

'Married?' He was listening intently.

'Widow. Eighteen months ago.'

'Oh.' He made the exclamation full of sympathy.

'She needs to work only from an interest point of view. Money is not a problem. She felt she needed a change of scene, without going too far away, and since we're on the Welsh Borders . . .'

'Sounds perfectly reasonable. You obviously think she'll fit in.'

'She was interested in the *practice*. I understood how she felt about responsibility. The pressures here are negligible after hospital life, and bereavement seems to follow a strange pattern—brings a restlessness after grief lessens. Obviously I didn't probe. She's dark, slim, strong personality. Mrs Boyer saw her, and thought she looked "sensible".'

Garth gave a broad grin. 'You haven't chosen an ugly duckling, by any chance?'

'Since you are so conceited!' she threw back at him. 'No, she is most attractive and certainly not a type ever to be overlooked.' As she talked, Andrea began to see the possible dangers of the situation. Suppose she and Nurse Drake shouldn't get on? Or, a small voice within her whispered, suppose Garth and she got on too well? A little shiver of apprehension touched her and, on its heels, a degree of ridicule, because it would not matter in the least if they did.

'Only the cliché that time will tell!' he observed with a smile.

'And the results be on my head,' she admitted.

'I could have got an assistant,' he prompted, reminding her of his earlier suggestion.

'I think we shall find that Nurse Drake will give us all the help we need at the moment.'

He held her gaze, again with a new assessment. 'You

can be very persuasive, Andrea.' He looked directly into her eyes, the gaze intensifying.

'Nature sometimes distributes her favours with discretion!' She glanced away swiftly, gave a little laugh, and sipped her drink.

'Where does our famous nurse propose to live, by the way?'

'She intends to buy something here, and in the meantime is staying in Darlbury Court, near me. They take two or three paying guests and have every facility.'

'I think there's something intriguing about Nurse Drake.'

'A young widow with money,' Andrea mused.

'Perfect for Romeos—of any age,' he laughed.

Andrea shook her head. 'I can't see her being easily fooled. She struck me as a person of excellent assessment.'

And on that observation, the subject was dropped.

It was an evening full of revelations; an exchange of views, the communication of two people establishing identity outside the realm of professionalism. The meal was perfect; the setting of the dining room, with its silver and cut glass, merely a natural manifestation of Garth's appreciation of beauty, and the dignity of the past. Yet, for all that, he would have been just as at home with a ploughman's lunch at a country inn. In many ways, Andrea thought as she listened to him, he was a contradiction. The atmosphere of the room, the Georgian windows, three panes across and four high, gave light to add to the sense of space. But in it all there was no woman's touch of any intimate nature, merely that provided by the expertise of Lily, who preferred to be called by her Christian name, but would have been slightly affronted had her husband not been given his rightful title.

'This has been a delicious meal,' Andrea said to Garth, when they were back in the sitting room having their coffee.

They both knew that words were floating above a sea of emotion; emotion that swirled about them, giving every look importance, every sudden silence an element of drama. They had come closer in the past hour or two than in the previous eighteen months.

'Have you seen much of Douglas?' Garth asked abruptly. 'Needed his help?'

'No, to both questions.'

Douglas Jayson was a close friend of Garth's. A serious type, a brilliant gynaecologist, who shared a house with his sister Natalie, whose forbidding personality made visiting them at West Close about as comfortable as sitting on a cactus. The picture was completed by their daily, Mrs Plum, a Dickensian character who shared Natalie's abhorrence of all modern amenities and thought that microwave ovens were an invention of the devil, calculated to poison the food.

Garth said frankly, 'Of course, Douglas is in love with you.'

Andrea gasped, '*What?*'

'Come now, you must know.'

'I most certainly don't!' she protested. 'Oh, we're friendly enough and get on . . .'

'As we have done?'

'I'm not involved with his work,' she countered. 'There is no analogy . . . Don't be silly!'

'Women are amazing creatures,' he said with a wry smile, 'and see only what they want to see.'

'Maybe. But I'll settle for a few more years of peace

and quiet. I'm not sexless, unromantic, or uninterested in men, but I'm enjoying emotional freedom,' she finished firmly. 'As for complications with Douglas . . . Can you imagine having Natalie for a sister-in-law? She'd dominate you!'

Garth laughed, 'I'd like to see anyone dominate *you*!' He held her gaze. 'It could be a splendid challenge, though.'

'And I don't want any challenges, either,' she insisted.

'I believe you,' he said quietly. 'I didn't realise you were such a complex character.' He paused, then continued, 'I'm sorry I cannot offer you another small brandy—you're driving.'

'In any case, I must be going.'

His gaze was direct and compelling as attraction held them. *Emotional freedom.* Her words echoed between them, bringing the very challenge she had also decried. Was it possible to be sexually immunised against a man whose every gesture she now found inviting?

To her surprise, he made no protest.

She got to her feet, aware of a chilling disappointment. Then, swiftly, as she walked towards the door, he reached her side and, with deliberation, put his arms round her and lowered his lips to hers, at first lightly and then with increasing passion. She felt rapture, sharp, exciting, stab her body, the pressure of his limbs awakening swift desire.

No words were spoken as he drew away, but his eyes looked deeply into hers as he then said with tantalising significance, 'I promise not to threaten your emotional freedom!'

With that, he opened the door and walked with her to her car.

Ludlow lay like a dark tapestry in the light of the

afterglow, the spacious town on the Welsh border rising above the Teme and the Corve, dating back to Norman times. The Butter Cross dominated Broad Street—an unusually wide impressive street—giving a suggestion of grandeur as, half-way down, lay the only survivor of Ludlow's six thirteenth-century gatehouses, upon the top of which a defiant eighteenth-century house was perched. Timber-framed buildings blended with elegant Georgian, while from it radiated little lanes and crooked dwellings, the upper storeys leaning over crazily, either not wishing to miss the grandeur of the scene, or bowing in reverence to it.

Andrea was blind to its familiar beauty as she drove through the medieval High Street, between the Castle and the Bull Ring. Her lips were still tingling from Garth's kiss, and the entire evening seemed rather like a fantasy. Garth, whom she had taken for granted, worked with, and felt secure with in the knowledge that they would never mix business with pleasure. Why, now, suddenly, this attraction? A short absence? She glanced across at the Castle which, even in its state of decay, still looked magnificent and imperious, its empty windows like dark sightless eyes. Finally, from the pavement in a quaint near-by street, she let herself into an ancient house in which she had a top-floor flat. A crooked narrow staircase led to its half-timbered sitting room. It was small, but full of character, and she had sustained its antiquity by the choice of a few carefully selected pieces of furniture—a monk's bench, a beautifully carved oak chest, comfortable chairs upholstered in ruby velvet, the colour and material duplicated in carpets and curtains, bringing the scene to life in rich contrast against the parchment panels in the sloping walls. She could see the Castle from a long narrow window (the other two being set precariously in the roof) half-way between floor and ceiling, which gave the effect of a permanent painting. A crescent moon beckoned, with Venus beside it, like a diamond cut in the sapphire May sky.

Without realising it, she hummed to herself as she prepared for bed in an attic room which she had transformed with Tudor Rose chintz, sofa table and tallboy.

Her last thought before falling asleep was whether engaging a nurse had been such a wise move, after all.

Andrea went into her consulting room the following morning as though seeing it for the first time. It was L-shaped, and provided excellent facility for an examining cubicle. Her desk was in front of the window, and Clare had already wheeled in the trolley on which all the necessary sterile instruments were arranged.

'No breathing-space this morning,' Clare said cheerfully, her round face and bright brown eyes almost angelic, but for the provocative smile that gave it a mischievous air.

'I've slipped in Stephanie Landon at one,' Andrea said, almost apologetically. 'But I'll let her in, so don't wait about in your lunch hour.' She went on, 'Although I know that half the time you cut it short if we're pushed . . . Ah, good morning,' she said to Garth, as he came through the open doorway.

Clare was on her way out.

'Give me three minutes, and then send the first patient in,' Andrea called to her.

'You've made this like a sitting room,' he observed. 'Those beautiful bird pictures, the photographs on the instrument cabinet . . . too few places like this around. Although I notice that I get flowers on my desk, these days!' He glanced at hers.

'Nothing to do with me,' she laughed. 'As for this room, it's as I arranged it when I came here.'

He drew her gaze to his. 'I've been pretty blind,' he said unexpectedly.

Surgery bell went.

'I'd like to play truant!' He walked to the door and looked back. 'How about having dinner at the Feathers this evening?' He shot the question at her.

'I'm going to the Mortimers for drinks.'

They were both remembering the kiss, and his eyes focused on her lips. Then, raising his glance, he exclaimed, 'So am I! I'd forgotten. We could have a meal afterwards'.'

She gave him a little smile. 'I never make plans for *after* a party . . . One gets caught up.'

'Fine,' he said confidently. 'I'll make sure *I* do the catching up.'

Andrea went through her appointment patients with their multifarious complaints, and just before one, Clare said, 'There's a cup of coffee ready, Dr Forbes, and a sandwich. We (meaning Mrs Boyer) thought you could manage it.' She added, 'Miss Landon can wait a minute or two!'

Andrea agreed.

Stephanie Landon was a slim, brown-haired girl who could have passed for at least eighteen. She normally had naturally flushed cheeks. Today, with a sense of shock, Andrea saw a pale shadow of the Stephanie she previously knew, and her heart contracted. Now she looked ill, and sinking gratefully into the patients' chair, she said hurriedly, before Andrea had time to do more than greet her, 'I'm not here to waste your time, Dr Forbes. I'm pregnant!'

Inwardly Andrea groaned, not feeling she could bear

another problematic abortion case. She didn't have time either to make a statement or to ask a question, as Stephanie hurried on, 'And I'm not here to plead for an abortion. I'm here to plead *not* to have one.'

The room held the silence of suspense; the walls leaned down oppressively to catch every word of the drama.

'Tell me about it,' Andrea said gently. 'And then let's see how I can help you.'

'It isn't a good thing to be old for one's years,' came the sighing announcement. 'You're neither child nor woman, but people talk to you as both. Men never *see* you as only fifteen. Then, when you tell them, they're shocked, and you lose their friendship. Equally, you have nothing whatever in common with boys of your own age. They seem like *children*! Boys are all younger than girls, at any age, anyway,' she observed sagely, and then gave Andrea the helpless pleading look of a wounded animal, as she added, 'My mother wants me to have an abortion—insists that I do, in fact; and I don't want one. Roy and I don't want one.'

This, Andrea thought, was a situation that didn't conform to the usual pattern.

'You cannot be forced to have an abortion, Stephanie.'

'You see, his parents run a dry cleaning business, and Roy, who is nineteen, works for them. He has ambition, and what Mummy can't forgive is that he isn't someone in *our* world. She forgets how Daddy started, and I hate the life we lead now. It's so unreal and artificial. People only like the money, the parties, my father's generosity . . . It's buying friendship, and I infuriate them because they say I haven't any ambition. They want me to move gracefully into a deb situation; see me with "the right people", whoever *they* may be,' she said bitterly.

Andrea knew that Stephanie was getting all the pent-up grievances out of her system, and prompted, 'Tell me about Roy?'

'I met him a year ago. I like sketching, and was doing a watercolour on the banks of the Teme, not far from the Linney leisure area. We noticed each other as we wandered around the beautiful building by the Castle grounds. We seemed to *know* each other, even then. I'd no idea of his age, or he mine, and when we did know, we agreed that it would make no difference. I took him home, and Mummy was so appallingly snooty and *patronising*. People ridicule childhood sweethearts, although we weren't quite that. We used to meet secretly, plan for the future. I know that sounds like the fairy story—the adolescent in the first ecstasy of love . . . If I talked like this to Mummy, she'd accuse me of reading romantic novels, even though she never reads anything herself.' She paused, sighed, looked down at her hands and then straight into Andrea's eyes. 'We made love nearly three months ago for the first time, having agreed that we wouldn't . . . I don't think that we either of us *realised* what was happening; everything overwhelmed us . . . Afterwards, I tried to tell myself that it wasn't often that virgins had babies the first time . . . Roy was horrified; blamed himself and never did it again. But I've missed two periods, been sick in the mornings—it was that.' She shook her head and covered her face with her hands. Then, 'Mummy realised, and got a urine test done . . . I'll never forget all the things she said to me—never. It was Roy's lack of money, his position, and the terror that anyone should know.'

Andrea sighed. She could imagine Myrna Landon and

her hopes of a millionaire son-in-law . . . Where would her friends be now?

'She says she can take me to London; that we can have a week there "shopping", and it can all be done quietly. There is someone she knows of . . . If I do this, she will not mention it again and I shall agree never to see Roy again. My father doesn't and mustn't, she insists, know.' The dark eyes widened in fear and appeal as she added, 'The alternative is that she will put the matter in the hands of the police, and Roy will be prosecuted because it would all come out anyway.' A great sob escaped her, and tears rolled down her cheeks as she cried, 'Oh, Dr Forbes, help me; help me! What can I do? We want the baby—in ten months we can marry. Roy isn't penniless, or without a job, and I have money that is my own, which Daddy gave me. I could have help . . .'

Andrea felt cold, despite the warmth of the day. She knew that Myrna Landon would agree to an illegal abortion rather than that her social structure should be flawed. The friends she cherished would not stand the test, and the dent in the family honour would smash all her carefully-thought-out plans for Stephanie's future. Andrea knew, too, that while she was Stephanie's doctor, she was helpless when it came to a mother's domination and authority.

'I'll never give our baby up—Never! Roy feels the same. No one will part us.'

'And Roy's parents?'

'They understand. They love each other,' she said simply. 'We neither of us expect people to think we were *right*. But if Roy were prosecuted . . . Don't you see?'

'Yes,' Andrea said, nodding. 'Perhaps, if I talked to your mother, I have some influence.'

Light, a glimmer of hope, made the tears shimmer again in appealing eyes.

'Oh, would you see her?'

'Most certainly . . . Oh, Stephanie, my dear, I'm so sorry you've had to go through all this.'

Stephanie cried, 'You're so *kind*, and Mummy has been so *cruel*. I'm not any of the things she says. Do you believe that young people can love and be faithful and stay married all their lives?' There was a pathetic note of pleading in the question.

Andrea didn't hesitate. 'Yes, I do. And I would add that there are many Golden Weddings to prove it. Equally, I would admit that very young love can be a tragedy and a bitter disillusionment—a disaster.'

There was no protest, but Stephanie said quietly, 'I've seen some disasters in the marriages of my school-friends' parents. I listen and I read. I can't help not thinking like some fifteen-year-old,' she said half-apologetically. 'And I'm not a stupid girl, wanting a baby, imagining that having it is going to be easy, or that Roy and I will live in some enchanted world. It won't be like that. But what we feel for each other is, well . . .' She broke off and lowered her gaze. 'You have to be in love, and *love* someone as a friend as well, before you can understand. That's why my mother has no idea of what all this means.' A flush crept up into her cheeks, and faint embarrassment betrayed itself. 'I know people would ridicule me and say I'm talking like an ignorant adolescent . . . but they still go to see *Romeo and Juliet*.'

Andrea had no answer to that.

'What we did was immature and irresponsible; we accept that, but we might have been in a trance, the emotion was so—so overwhelming.'

Andrea sat listening, aware that she was dealing with

something she herself had never experienced. Flirtations, yes; all the inconsequential relationships; but never anything deep or serious. Garth's kiss had made the greatest impact, and she didn't seek to deny it.

Stephanie went on, 'How can I convince anyone that, despite what's happened, Roy is old for his age, and serious? Nothing would induce him to love me in that way again—even though, now, it wouldn't matter. You've no idea how he condemns himself.'

Andrea nodded, her silence full of understanding sympathy. Then she said, 'There's the question of your school—you're at Greystone—not boarding.'

'Yes, but I'm going to board in September . . .' She corrected herself, 'I was going to do so . . .' She gave a little strangled cry that trailed off into a pathetic wail. 'Oh, I *know* how all this will affect my life . . .'

'And the baby, Stephanie,' Andrea prompted gently.

'It will have two loving parents and two loving grandparents. My mother will never want to see me again if I don't give way to her.' There was a moment of poignant silence during which Stephanie's courage ebbed, and she said shakenly, 'As I talk to you, it all seems so *sad*. A baby causing all this.' She looked down at her hands, her face in shadow, and then said with an almost frightening calm, 'A few minutes out of one's life—one wrong thing.'

Andrea thought desperately that to ask someone of experience to make such an emotive decision would be traumatic, but to expect a fifteen-year-old girl to do so seemed more like a crucifixion, no matter how mature she might be. But neither thoughts nor words could solve the problem. She said with a feeling of inner desperation, her voice gentle, but serious, 'The responsibility of a child and a wife for a young man of nineteen is a very grave one, Stephanie. And you have to think of all it would entail so far as you were concerned. They are factors to be weighed up.' She added, 'It's your whole life . . .'

No protest came at first, and then words tumbled out. 'You see, my mother hasn't talked to me like this: everything has been from her point of view and the ghastly social aspect.' There was a note of anguish in her cry, 'I only know that I don't want an abortion. Oh, I'm not blind; I see the advantages, and that it would be the easiest way out.' She paused. 'If my relationship with Roy were some irresponsible flirtation—just sex—it would be different.' Her voice dropped. 'Being wrong and foolish once, doesn't mean that you're like that all the time.' Her hands clenched in her lap. 'I don't know what to do, even so. I couldn't bear to wreck Roy's life, his future; to become a burden. He could blame me afterwards for not doing as . . . when the baby was really here—' She looked solemn as she asked suddenly, unexpectedly, a strange far-away look in his eyes, 'Do you believe that time heals? Or is that just another cliché?'

Andrea answered resolutely, 'I know that time heals because I have evidence of it every day in my profession. The confusion arises when it comes to forgetting . . . But memories can be treasured long after grief has gone.' Her tone became earnest. 'If that were not true, life could not go on, and no one would have a second chance of happiness.'

Stephanie nodded, her eyes wide, her expression that of acceptance. 'And everything I've said here is in confidence?' The question came abruptly.

'Absolute confidence in all circumstances.'

Stephanie glanced at her watch and got to her feet. It

seemed utterly ludicrous that she was returning to school.

'Thank you, Dr Forbes, for being so kind—for *listening*. I don't think it would help for you to see my mother, and she'd hate me even more because I'd confided in you. I'm the only one who can make the decision, after all, no matter what is said.'

Andrea told her urgently. 'Keep in touch.' She scribbled the telephone number of her flat on a card. 'Ring me at home—any time—and if Roy would like to talk to me . . . well, you know where to find me.'

Stephanie was on the verge of tears as they walked to the front door and she stepped out on to the pavement. There was a choking sensation in Andrea's throat as she watched the dejected figure disappear from view.

Garth came through from the dining room as Andrea shut the front door.

'Join me for a coffee?' He looked at her speculatively. 'And what did you do about lunch?'

She told him.

'Then another coffee won't be amiss,' he insisted as they went into the sitting room together. 'I suppose we must go to the Mortimers?' he said, when they were settled. His gaze was steady and unnerving, and they both knew that a fierce sexual attraction was pleading its own cause.

'It would be very rude not to do so unless we had an emergency.'

'So we can't win either way!' he said whimsically.

There was a bold determination in his attitude that suggested that explanations were unnecessary and that she understood his language and its innuendo.

'I won't threaten your emotional freedom, I promise.'

His words re-echoed, and she felt that he had already

done so, since his voice, his presence, his entire personality thrilled and dominated her.

She said rashly, the words tumbling out involuntarily, 'I'll vie with Lily and cook you a meal one evening. You've been to my flat, but you've never *seen* it: you came in like a whirlwind to drag me off to a difficult midder.'

'I'm not aware of having had any previous invitation,' he pointed out.

'Then I'm making up for the omission.'

'When?' he demanded.

'Next Tuesday? Nurse Drake will have started on the Monday.'

'Tuesday?' He flicked his diary from his pocket, studied it, and said, 'Fine. I shall look forward to it.'

'You could almost put my flat into your dining room and this room,' she said.

'I'm not coming to study the flat . . . How did you get on with Stephanie?'

She explained the circumstances.

'That's typical of Myrna Landon,' he said. 'Why the hell didn't she come to you?'

'Because I should always have been a reminder. This must be done as though it had never happened. She has a valid point of view, but it is the *way* she has gone about it; her attitude to the girl. The whole thing could be built up into a tragedy.'

'Young love,' he said quietly.

'All love,' she added. 'The heights and the depths.'

'Is it because you recognise this that you want emotional freedom?' He added, 'A basic fear?' He was studying her as he spoke, and seeming to hang upon her answer.

'Perhaps. And *this* won't see the patients. I've an

emphysema, a coronary visit, a bad dose of 'flu . . . Oh, and a miscarriage that got me out in the night! Must satisfy myself about that. And I've got to check old Mrs Brown's blood pressure. At eighty-five, she seems as fit as a fiddle, but one can't take chances.'

'Not when one eventually has to sign the death certificate. Strange, isn't it, though, how we hate to lose our patients. We can joke . . .'

'We'd go berserk if we couldn't!'

They looked at each other, suddenly silent, aware of how much they had in common and how closely their views were identified.

As Andrea stood up, the telephone rang. Garth leaned forward and pressed his lips to hers before answering it. His hand gripped hers. There was a magnetism in his touch, the thrill of anticipation in his manner.

She heard his attractive voice saying, 'Dr Howard speaking . . . Yes, Mrs Somerton,' and felt a curious and unexpected involvement. Noreen Somerton had a terrific crush on Garth, and, for the first time, Andrea was aware of faint sympathy. It struck her that he must be a pretty devastating man to have as a doctor. A curious sensation of satisfaction touched her because their own present relationship was exactly what she desired: he understood her outlook, which precluded any pretence.

Andrea greeted Nurse Drake (Elaine to her friends), the following Monday morning, with a feeling of relief tempered with faint apprehension lest Garth might not be wholly satisfied with her choice.

Elaine Drake was taller than Andrea, and more self-assertive. She had an air of one accustomed to giving orders, and was highly professional in everything she did. Her oval face was arresting, the expression at times soft, almost enticing, then hard and determined; her skin was tanned, her eyes blue and discerning.

'I came in early,' she explained to Andrea, 'and have had a session with Mrs Boyer and Clare. I want to familiarise myself with the patients' names and complaints, so that I require as little briefing as possible. You and Dr Howard want help, not hindrance! All I hope is that he will approve of me.'

'So do I!' Andrea said jokingly.

'When do I meet him?' The question was asked lightly, but there was anticipation and a certain eagerness behind it.

'Now,' Andrea replied. 'Come with me.' She led her to Garth's consulting room, opened the door, and said brightly, 'Dr Howard, here is our new nurse—Nurse Drake.'

Elaine's face was almost blank as she went forward. No sign of nervousness betrayed itself as she said, before Garth had time to speak, 'I hope I shall not be too much of a disappointment, Dr Howard.'

There was a second of dramatic silence. Andrea was struck by the almost frozen expression of what might have been termed disbelief on Garth's face, as though, even in a split second, he thoroughly disapproved of the girl now facing him.

CHAPTER TWO

ANDREA watched Garth get to his feet, move from his desk and extend his hand, his manner stiff, his expression inscrutable, as he said, 'Good morning, Nurse Drake.' Then, as though aware of his abruptness, he continued, 'I hope we shall all be able to work together amicably.'

'He's certainly not making any concessions,' Andrea thought wryly, and felt a wave of apprehension, unable to fathom Garth's reaction. He was normally a friendly person who, while jealously guarding his private world, nevertheless put everyone at their ease

She noticed the rather surprised expression in Nurse Drake's eyes as she answered, 'I'm sure we shall.' A little of her confidence had evaporated.

Andrea left them.

As the door closed, Garth said without preliminaries, 'Whatever are *you* doing here, Elaine? Why couldn't you have contacted me direct?'

'Because, when I found out that you were away, I thought it would be better to present you with a *fait accompli*, so that you could not have any second thoughts. Also, I felt I could plead my cause better this way.'

'"Cause"?' He was immediately uneasy and suspicious.

She sighed deeply. 'I need a friend, Garth. Dr Forbes will have told you that I lost my husband eighteen months ago . . .' Her voice trailed away as she sat down in the patients' chair, and he returned to his desk. Before he could make any comment, she rushed on, 'I don't want anyone to know about the past. No shadows. Yesterday is always a lost cause. I'd just begun to re-adjust my life and had been married for only a year, when Ralph, my husband, died.'

Garth cut in, 'I'm sorry; but none of this really concerns me. I agree that yesterday is a lost cause, so why couldn't you leave it at that? I'm sure you have plenty of friends.'

Elaine's heart missed a beat. It was vital to convince him. 'I have friends, yes, but no one I can trust or who would ever understand. You're different. You must appreciate that.'

He protested, his voice firm, his expression warning, 'Your coming here is utterly fantastic in the circumstances.'

'It might also be argued that it is natural . . . Oh, Garth, please understand? I don't want to interfere with your life in any way, or to drag up the past. In fact, I ask for your assurance that it shall never be mentioned. All I want is to work for you. I like Dr Forbes, and I'm more than capable of filling the post. I've never thought of your being prejudiced.' She looked softly pleading. 'It would mean everything in the world to be part of all this . . . Give life a purpose.' She watched him carefully, knowing that he always appreciated reason and was basically soft-hearted. 'I wouldn't intrude, or ask any favours. I just want to belong somewhere, and your interests would be mine.'

'That all sounds valid,' he agreed, unconvinced. 'But I don't want yesterday to be a shadow . . .' He got up from his chair restlessly. 'It would have to be a clean slate, and you would have to behave as my employee, as though we had just met. In which case, I fail to see how your cause, as you call it, would be served.'

She lowered her eyes and her long lashes shadowed her cheek; there was a rather pathetic, lost look about her.

'I should be here; secure in a job that meant something. There'd be no harm in trying.'

'It's all so unreal,' he exclaimed a little explosively.

'You can apply that word to life generally,' she said. 'We could so easily have met by coincidence.'

'But this isn't coincidence.'

'No,' she said with an honesty that was not lost on him. 'Doctors are easily traced, particularly those advertising for a nurse . . . Well, I am a nurse.' Her gaze met his. 'I'd like to have your friendship. So much has happened in the past five years since I saw you last. My whole life has changed. I'm Mrs Drake.' She paused, and shook her head. 'If you only knew how I need to belong somewhere—even if it is only in a job. I can't cope with hospital life any more. Oh, Garth, don't you see?'

'Yes,' he said quietly, despite himself touched by her frankness. He was silent for a second, then, 'Suppose we take it from here?' The words came swiftly, 'Since you have the job anyway.'

Elaine smoothed one hand over the other and then looked at him with obvious gratitude. 'We'll make a pact never to mention the past to anyone, or to discuss it.'

'That above all and, essentially, we'd be honest with each other if we ever wanted to change that pattern.'

'If you knew what being able to come here means to me!' Her voice was shaking. 'Thank you. Just *thank you*!'

She sat there, looking appealing in her uniform and knowing it, but, as she got to her feet, her manner altered. 'And now, Dr Howard, I'll begin work.' She thought in that second that he didn't seem to have changed, unless it was to have become more attractive —a more powerful and magnetic personality. In turn, Garth appreciated that she appeared younger than her thirty years, and that her charm lay in a certain vulnerability, which softened a manner that could be authoritative.

Elaine went back to Mrs Boyer's office. The secretary took off her typing spectacles and let them hang like a necklace. Efficiency was stamped on her features like make-up. Her hair was short, slightly curly, and an indeterminate brown; her features sharp, eyes direct and, on occasion, piercing. Elaine had already summed her up, and the picture she now presented was the antithesis of that shown to Garth.

'A sound, no-nonsense man, your Dr Howard,' Elaine exclaimed deliberately, knowing that Mrs Boyer would suspect, and disapprove of, any flamboyant adjectives with a sexual connotation.

Mrs Boyer smiled. Nurse Drake would do. She had common sense.

Clare joined them. She reserved judgment on Elaine, whom she considered to be far away from her age-group and not like Dr Forbes, who was part of the modern scene. But she said pleasantly, 'Your first patient is waiting.' Elaine had been allocated a small room off Andrea's. 'A Mrs Bright,' Clare added, 'whose religion is her blood pressure, and she thinks it should be checked like the time. As she's over eighty, we humour her! Dr Howard is very kind to old ladies and animals!'

'*Really*, Clare!' Mrs Boyer admonished, flicking her spectacles back into position and typing again furiously.

Meanwhile Andrea was trapped by Mrs Keen, a

menopausal woman who read books on the change of life with the same relish as children consumed Smarties. She 'knew it all', and treated her hot flushes as an illness, driving her family to despair. She was allergic to hormone therapy and haunted the surgery.

Andrea said in desperation, 'Have you ever thought of trying homoeopathy?'

Mrs Keen echoed the word as a shriek, adding, '*You* a *doctor* suggesting such a thing! I don't approve of . . .'

'We keep an open mind about anything that might benefit our patients,' Andrea cut in.

The telephone rang: an urgent call, which Mrs Boyer had switched through.

Andrea heard Myrna Landon's hysterical voice calling, 'Oh, Dr Forbes, please come . . . We've just found Stephanie . . . An accident in the swimming pool!'

Andrea was on her feet even as she replaced the receiver, saying, 'I'm sorry, Mrs Keen—an emergency. Forgive me.' She grabbed her medical bag, hurried through to Mrs Boyer, gave her instructions and was away in a matter of a minute.

'*Stephanie . . . An accident in the swimming pool!*' Andrea's thoughts raced with the car as it sped a little way out of town on the Knighton Road to a large white house that looked exactly like a film-set. Rhododendrons and azaleas flanked the drive to the colonnaded entrance and front door, where Myrna Landon and her husband (a plump man, now ashen-faced) stood agitatedly. She did the talking in staccato sentences, as they made their way down a long wide corridor, thickly carpeted in royal blue and flower-decked, to the swimming pool. 'We assumed she'd gone to school . . . We were late up this morning; and then Reynolds (their factotum) mentioned that she'd not had any breakfast, or been seen.'

Stephanie was lying on the tiled surround of the pool under one of the gaily striped umbrellas, covered with a large royal blue bath-towel. Rigor mortis had not yet set in, and after a brief examination, Andrea removed her stethoscope and said, 'She has probably been dead for about two hours.'

Myrna Landon's voice was high-pitched, shocked. 'We thought she was playing truant, that's why we *looked* here!'

'You spoke of an accident,' Andrea prompted.

Only then did Myrna Landon show the fear that was making her feel sick. 'Well, it's obviously an accident,' she insisted. 'I mean . . .'

Harvey Landon cried in distress, 'She was such a good swimmer—she loved swimming and usually had an early dip.'

Myrna Landon looked at Andrea, half in apprehension, half in hope. 'You *know* her; I mean, you . . .' She floundered.

'I can only tell you that she is dead, Mrs Landon. There will have to be a post-mortem before the actual cause can be established.'

'"Post-mortem"! But—' the voice rose on a shrill note of desperation, 'drowning is simple enough; it's obviously an accident, and . . .'

'And a case for the police, I'm afraid.' Andrea shook her head.

'But you—*you* know us, and—' the voice rose again, 'she was a normal happy girl, without a care in the world.'

'Then that will be established at the inquest,' Andrea said quietly, realising that Myrna Landon was never going to betray the fact that she knew of her daughter's pregnancy.

'Dr Forbes is quite right,' Harvey put in dully. 'We're as much in the dark as anyone. I tried artificial respiration while my wife telephoned, but I knew it was useless, although there was not much water.'

Andrea didn't explain that, in some cases of drowning, there wasn't enough water swallowed to kill the victim by displacing air from the lungs because a reflex keeps the larynx closed against the water, therefore it is a question of choking. Also, that the muscles of the throat relax soon after consciousness is lost, and that is why, if given a chance to breath, life is saved.

'I'm deeply sorry,' Andrea said helplessly.

'But couldn't you do something? I mean, need there be . . . ?' Myrna Landon's eyes were now wide with near-terror.

'I've done all I'm empowered to do in the circumstances,' Andrea said, a great sadness lying like a weight on her heart. 'I'll ring the police.' She sighed. 'We have quite a bit to do with them, one way and another.'

And even as she did so, Andrea was aware of the luxury surrounding her: the expensive tables and chairs in dazzling white against pale blue tiles. The high-domed ceiling; smooth sliding doors leading to a wide patio that took up half of one side of the house . . . And Stephanie's still, lonely tragic figure lying under its covering, mocking everything around her. Andrea heard the echo of all that had been said a matter of days ago: the pathos of it all; and, as she looked at Myrna Landon, she resented bitterly the confidentiality which forbade her making any challenge, any accusation. There was no doubt in her own mind that Stephanie had taken her own life . . . Her words, *'Do you believe that time heals?'* Was she, even then, thinking of Roy, planning what she would do—the alternatives being more than she could bear?

'Oh God,' Harvey Landon cried suddenly, brokenly. 'It's like a nightmare.' He seemed to have shrunk, his grief deep and baffled.

Andrea waited until the police arrived, and had a word with the superintendent, whom she knew.

'Thank you, Dr Forbes,' Superintendent Knight said when Andrea had given him the details.

'You know where to find me,' she told him, their eyes meeting in understanding.

Finally she left the flower-filled white house, dazed, choked, and thankful that she had not been involved in any way with Stephanie's pregnancy, or even examined her. Their conversation was as sacred as one that took place in the confessional.

Elaine met her on her return to Clee View. 'My goodness, you look shocked, Dr Forbes!'

'I *feel* shocked.'

Elaine said with understanding, 'I'll get you a coffee. Dr Howard has seen your last two patients.'

Andrea returned to reality. 'How did you get on with Dr Howard, by the way?'

Elaine smiled. 'I think I won his cautious approval in the end.'

'Oh, good! Now we're both on solid ground . . . I *would* be grateful for that coffee.' She added, 'Tell Clare to make it extra strong, and I'll have it black.' Garth's name echoed and seemed a panacea. But, Andrea told herself, she was a doctor, and nothing—neither death, birth, accidents nor suicides—could be allowed to interfere with the discipline demanded. There was no time to indulge in prolonged sadness for one patient when another was waiting. Nevertheless, her eyes were moist. She prayed that death would be kind . . .

Morning surgery finished, Garth strode into Andrea's consulting room a little later. He never seemed to *enter* a room, but rather to take possession of it, as she stepped over the threshold.

'What happened?' he asked anxiously.

She gave him the details.

'Suicide?'

'I can see no other possibility. I shan't forget Mrs Landon talking of her being a happy girl without a care in the world. Whatever the case, she will plead ignorance and play the devastated mother. Sympathetic publicity. And there's bound to be the maximum of that. The family is news. The son, Malcolm, is in America, apparently.' Andrea paused. 'I'm deeply sorry for him and for the father, but I must admit to feeling very harsh towards the mother. The last time I treated Stephanie professionally was for 'flu in January.' Her gaze met Garth's with significance. 'My evidence concerns that occasion, and pronouncing her dead. I'm thankful I had not been consulted about her physical condition, or even examined her—nothing in relationship to the pregnancy.'

'Coroners are there to get at the facts,' Garth reminded her.

'My facts are embodied in the oath I took when I became a doctor. Only you, as my partner, are allowed any discussion. I'm sure of one thing: Myrna Landon is tormented by what she *wonders* I may know; and she dares not ask me. Her husband knows nothing. The shock is great now, but it will be far greater.'

Silence fell, and Andrea brought the conversation back to their own affairs.

'I understand you've accepted Nurse Drake? She said she felt she had won your "cautious approval". I must say you didn't give her an exactly enthusiastic welcome.' Andrea hesitated. 'You looked as though you were meeting someone of whom you already disapproved.'

'Nonsense!' Garth retorted. 'She just wasn't what I expected!' The words, he thought, couldn't have been more true.

'And definitely not the ugly duckling?' Andrea smiled.

'No. I agree that she is very keen to work here.' Garth disliked the falseness of his position intensely. The pact with Elaine, not to divulge the facts, seemed suddenly fraught with danger. Inwardly he cursed the sudden complication that challenged his previous peace of mind. It seemed important not to have any secrets from Andrea.

And, despite Garth's reassurance, Andrea was aware of a faint apprehension. In some strange way Nurse Drake's name held significance as though her presence was already like a stone thrown into still waters.

'I don't want to have any doubts, Garth,' she burst out. 'We've too much work to have to think of personalities. Did you make any arrangements about the time factor?'

He avoided evasion by saying, 'We agreed to take it from here. You need have no qualms: you were absolutely right to engage her in the circumstances. I'm sure she will live up to all your professional expectations.' He felt the remark needed a rider. 'If my enthusiasm hasn't quite matched your own, it is only because I am jealous of our present harmony in the practice and want to preserve it.'

Andrea relaxed and murmured, 'I share your reactions.'

Their awareness of each other suddenly took precedence; his gaze held hers, bringing sudden tension and an electric silence.

'What time tomorrow evening?' he asked hoarsely and irrelevantly, and with sudden urgency.

'About seven-thirty?'

The intercom went.

'Yes, Nurse,' Andrea said pleasantly. 'By all means come in now.'

Garth cursed under his breath, but remained until Elaine joined them, asking deliberately, 'How did it go?'

Andrea was glad that Garth's tone was friendly.

'Splendidly. I spared you quite a few malingerers; dressed an ulcer and arranged for a nurse to call as a follow-up. The sphygmomanometer has worked overtime. Old Mrs Bright was quite disappointed when I said that her blood pressure was normal. She retorted, "Ah, but only because of the Propranolol tablets!" I'll watch that it doesn't drop further, so that she might get giddy.' She rushed on, 'After the bustle of hospital, this is like a holiday!'

Andrea was a little surprised by the ease with which she talked to Garth as she stood there, adding as she addressed him, 'I shouldn't be surprised if the spiky-haired Donald Maddox has glandular fever . . .'

Andrea interposed, 'Glandular fever is very often indistinguishable from other respiratory infections.'

'That's true,' Garth agreed.

'I could be wrong,' Elaine said, 'but somehow I don't think I am. He was quite ill; no appetite, a headache . . . Your patient, Dr Forbes. We arranged that you would call.' She looked first at Garth and then back to Andrea. 'I consulted Dr Howard in your absence.'

Garth nodded his agreement.

Andrea felt irritated by her own reactions. Nurse Drake might have been there a year instead of a few hours.

'Mrs Boyer said you could fit the visit in about three this afternoon.'

'I'm seeing Mrs Grimsby——' Andrea began.

'Mrs Grimsby cancelled; she has a very bad cold,' Elaine explained. She looked at Garth, and asked smoothly, 'Will you want me to attend while you examine Mrs Richey this afternoon, Dr Howard? She's a new patient.'

There was a strange, rather uneasy, silence. Andrea studied Garth's face, but his expression was coolly professional as he said, 'Yes, Nurse. Thank you for mentioning it.'

'Instinct, after hospital life,' Elaine said easily. 'Chaperoning the consultants . . .' She laughed, 'And some of them need it!' Immediately she had spoken, she seemed to draw a mask over her face, and squaring her shoulders, said with a certain deference, 'I think that is all. I'm now going to study the appointments list for this evening's surgery. Mrs Boyer and Clare have been most helpful.'

'Would you give Mrs Boyer these letters?' Garth said, handing her several. 'I have signed them.'

She took them, and went swiftly from the room, her manner wholly business-like.'

'Efficient,' said Andrea, without knowing why she suddenly felt irritated.

'Nurse Drake is not the type to miss much,' Garth observed, but it was the observation of experience.

'She was certainly very definite over Donald Maddox. I hope he hasn't glandular fever. He's just started as a singer with a pop group, and has aspirations in that direction.' Andrea spoke with feeling. She saw beneath the spiky, gelled hair, and always wondered why the older generation condemned pop, without remembering the jitterbug and, earlier, the charleston.

Garth looked at her with admiration. 'I like your humanist approach to things and people,' he said, adding unguardedly, 'I don't think you'll find that quality in Nurse Drake—professionally, at least,' he hastened.

Andrea said immediately, 'You seem to have summed her up pretty swiftly.'

'That doesn't mean I shall be proved right.' He paused, lowered his gaze and shifted his weight from one foot to the other. 'I think it would be as well if we didn't introduce any social element into the relationship. Keep things on a purely business-like footing. It's easier to get involved than to extricate oneself.' He stopped rather awkwardly. 'For a minute,' he went on, 'I'd forgotten that I was talking to someone who avoids involvement!'

Andrea had cause to remember his words.

'I was talking about an entirely different facet of life on that occasion.' She studied him intently. 'Having accepted Nurse Drake, why should you make such a resolve after knowing her for merely a matter of hours?'

Garth lowered his gaze and then raised it, looking at Andrea almost challengingly, 'Shall we put it down to man's intuition?'

'Together with the obvious assumption that Nurse Drake would be more than ready to indulge in social contacts?'

Garth knew that he had handled the matter clumsily, and looked awkward as he countered, 'I was considering the matter wholly from our point of view.'

She disarmed him by saying reasonably, 'I agree with you; but it isn't always so easy when one's contacts with a person are very much on an equal footing.'

Garth, relieved, nevertheless echoed, 'No. It isn't easy at all.'

Andrea stared at him. There was a note of depression in his voice which she could not understand. She did not want to admit that she was already a little bewildered by Garth's reactions, but consoled herself that it followed the consistency of the pattern—he had not wanted *any* nurse in the first place!

Andrea saw Donald Maddox that afternoon. His father was a master carpenter, and the family had a small half-timbered cottage tucked away in Corve Street, which had been vastly improved by Jo Maddox's skills. Donald was an only child whose way-out appearance and interests in no way put him in the drug scene or among the hooligan brigade. His parents, wisely, were his friends, not his critics. He had a good voice, and it was up to him what he did with it. His friends' 'group' was already getting known, with a few local bookings at various functions and discos, and their aims were high. Donald had a regular girl-friend, and his parents had no desire to sweep her into the cupboard, or under the carpet, rather than admit that they intermittently lived together. There was more loyalty and fidelity between them than in many modern marriages.

'Donald's very hot,' Edna Maddox, his mother, said as she took Andrea upstairs. 'So good of you to call, Doctor, and so quickly. He felt pretty rough when he got to surgery this morning, and he doesn't make a fuss

—not like his father,' she added with a little giggle. She was a comfortably plump little woman like a cosy armchair, and Andrea liked her. The cottage was spotless, and there was happiness in the atmosphere. 'Jenny's sitting with him. He was thankful to crawl to bed when he got home after surgery.' Jenny was his girlfriend, whom Andrea knew.

'Sorry, Doctor,' Donald croaked weakly. His hair now had a tired look which was rather incongruous, his face was flushed, his temperature high. 'Like Mum says, I feel rough.' In fact, he never quite knew how he had driven to the surgery that morning, except through sheer will-power.

'You should have sent for me,' Andrea said sympathetically, and made a thorough examination. His tonsils were inflamed, the glands in his neck slightly enlarged, but there was no swelling in either his groin or underarms; neither was the spleen palpable, and there was no evidence of glandular fever.

'I must be OK next week . . . There's this gig.' His dark-rimmed eyes looked fearfully into hers.

'You've tonsillitis,' she said. 'The worst should be over in forty-eight hours, with plenty of fluids and pain-killers.' She added cheerfully, 'You should be able to make your show.'

'Oh, great!' he whispered, his young face creasing into a smile.

'This is infectious,' she warned him, 'but more so in the early stages. Unfortunately, antibiotics do not cure it.'

'Mum and Jen?'

'We'll keep our fingers crossed.' Andrea added, 'I'm going to take a swab.'

'Ugh!'

'Precautionary. You're in good shape generally, Donald. Splendid.' She closed her medical bag a few minutes later. 'I'll look in tomorrow,' she promised. 'Now I'll have a word with your mother.'

He nodded, and as she turned away, gratefully closed his eyes.

Andrea reassured Mrs Maddox, instructing her to give him plenty of fruit juices and not to worry about his eating. 'He won't feel like food, and it won't hurt him to go without. He's strong and will soon throw this off.'

Jenny Broughton hovered near by as they stood on the small landing, wide-eyed and obviously worried. She was a size ten, and had a child-like appeal with her flaxen hair in studied disarray, tight jeans and a loose shirt tracing the lines of her near-perfect figure.

'Pain-killers,' Andrea added. 'Have you any?'

'Yes, some Paracetamol,' Mrs Maddox said. 'You prescribed them for my husband's headaches. But he's better now.'

'Give Donald two every four hours. I'll look in tomorrow. Since antibiotics won't cure the complaint, I see no purpose in their use.'

'What with the side-effects,' Mrs Maddox said knowledgeably. 'Made me that ill when I had them once—you remember?'

Andrea nodded and edged her way down the stairs.

'He *will* be all right?' Jenny asked as they reached the front door. 'I mean he looked so ill . . . Madness to have gone to surgery, but men won't listen, Doctor, will they?'

'No, they won't listen; but we'll have him fit for the end of next week.'

Relief mingled with what was a wide trusting smile.

'You've been so good to us, Doctor,' Mrs Maddox said spontaneously. 'When Jo had pneumonia . . .'

Andrea opened the front door herself. It was easier to get into a patient's house than out of it!

Elaine heard the result of the visit with frank surprise, and persisted, 'Glandular fever can sometimes follow on from tonsillitis, of course.'

Andrea pulled rank. 'Yes, Nurse Drake, I am aware of that, but you must leave the diagnosis to me.'

Elaine flushed. It was not going to be as easy as she thought to play the part of a subordinate to Garth's partner.

Andrea selected a meal of Ogen melon, cold salmon and peaches in brandy for Garth the following evening. It was simple; prepared in advance so that conversation would not be interrupted by visits to the kitchen. With it she chose a Bâtard Montrachet. The dining table (covered with a fine linen and lace tablecloth that had belonged to her grandmother) was circular and laid with Princes Plate cutlery and Cabinet glass, its two silver candlesticks—divided by a bowl of lilies of the valley to avoid the blocking of view by tall flowers—completed an artistic picture, and she stood back and looked at it all with a degree of pride. She didn't want to build the evening up, or give Garth's visit undue importance, she told herself, but nothing could stop the excitement that was increasing her normal heart-beat. The small room, sunlit, whispered of yesterday, with its beams and the rocking-chair standing by the chimney corner.

Garth was there punctually at seven-thirty, and even as he stepped over the threshold, the telephone rang.

'Oh, *no*!' They spoke in chorus.

But it was Douglas Jayson, apologising for his silence and explaining that he'd been at a medical conference in London for the past two days. Would she have dinner with him tomorrow at the Feathers? 'I know it's short notice,' he hastened, 'but it seems I've been away for years. I suppose you're not free tonight, by any chance?'

Andrea raised her voice slightly so that Garth, who had walked tactfully into the sitting room, should hear.

'Sorry, Douglas, tonight is not possible. Tomorrow, yes.'

'You're not alone,' he said.

'No.'

'Oh . . . Tomorrow, then. I'll pick you up at seven.'

Andrea, tantalisingly so far as Garth was concerned, joined him, saying only, 'Sorry about that. One always thinks it is a patient.' She indicated the drinks tray. 'Will you . . . ?'

He moved towards it. 'The Tio Pepe?'

She nodded, indicating the decanter.

'I'll join you.' He poured out the sherries and put the glasses down on side-tables by the arms of their respective chairs. There was a certain formality about him at that moment.

Andrea watched him warily as she sat down. He was wearing a cream linen jacket, dark grey trousers and white shirt. It was impossible to accept his presence without being aware of a curious suspense.

They raised their glasses, looked at each other, and sipped.

'This is a unique flat,' he said, glancing round him. 'You've given it character and personality.' His gaze was steady. 'Not surprising, since you have both.'

'Thank you.' She smiled, relaxing. 'After Clee View, it is just a box-room! But all I need, and I'm happy here.'

'"Happy"!' he echoed. 'What a vast word that is. And it means something different to each one of us.'

Andrea laughed. 'You sound like an old man!'

Garth thought of recent events. 'I can feel like an old man, on occasion.'

Andrea flashed him a meaning smile. 'I've no intention of entertaining an old man this evening. So I warn you!'

'Or you'll invite Douglas to take my place.' The words were out before he knew it.

'Quite probably.'

'You're an enigma, Andrea.'

'Better than being an open book!'

'May I ask how friendly you are with Douglas?' His voice was serious. 'I've already told you that he is in love with you!'

She said swiftly, 'My relationship with Douglas is as platonic as any man–woman friendship.'

'That's a pretty open-ended assertion, and it doesn't preclude emotional involvement.'

Andrea looked at him with a provocative directness. 'When I have an emotional involvement with anyone, Garth, the chances are you'll be the first to know.'

And even as she spoke, she was being drawn to him irresistibly, inexorably, excitement like a fire within her. He was obviously interested in her friendships, or his reaction to Douglas would not have been so immediate.

There was a sudden heavy silence. Deliberately he got to his feet and crossed to her chair, sitting on the arm of it, holding her gaze with a passion that darkened his eyes, as he whispered hoarsely, 'Heaven knows I'm involved with *you*.' And, with that, his lips went down fiercely on hers.

CHAPTER THREE

As Andrea's lips parted to meet his, the thrill of his touch brought an ecstasy and awareness of the passion rising between them. It was only when, breathless, she drew back, that she realised the excitement of a new and unfamiliar happiness. She had no wish to question or analyse, and ignored his remark about involvement, saying, 'Let me keep my head until we've eaten!'

He countered swiftly, 'Does that imply a readiness to lose it afterwards?' He got up and moved away, his timing impeccable: to have prolonged that particular moment would have been to make it an issue and rob it of its magic.

Their eyes met, the gaze lingering. Her smile was intriguing. 'Taking a moment at a time has possibilities. Planning so often falls short of expectations!' She sipped her sherry as though the interlude was natural and needed no further comment.

Garth's expression was slightly baffled. He found it extremely difficult to sum Andrea up. Actually, beneath her outward calm, there was emotional turmoil. No man had roused her in this way before, and she had never been so conscious of a sexual attraction which gave every movement significance. His strong physical appeal was enhanced by a sensitivity and appreciation of the fitness of things.

Later, he followed her out into the kitchen with ease and naturalness, opened the wine, and then lit the red candles on the dining table.

'This is a wonderful idea of yours,' he said, not having attempted to introduce any note of intimacy which would have diminished the importance of his kiss.

'No hovering waiters to interrupt the conversation!' she said with a smile.

'And we've a great deal of conversation to catch up on,' he suggested ungrammatically. 'I don't know nearly enough about you.'

They started their melon.

'There is very little to tell . . . We would both appear to have led very conventional lives. Unless, of course,' she added provocatively, 'impressions are deceptive, and you've a dark secret lurking in the cupboard.'

Silence fell before he replied, 'If any doctor can escape publicity . . .' He lowered his gaze, raised it and, changing the subject, asked with a degree of banality, 'Did you always want to go in for medicine?'

Andrea was not lost to his faint embarrassment, and felt a little wave of apprehension. Why bring the word 'publicity' into it? Her original remark had merely implied that his life had been free from complications, like her own. His appeal seemed to increase and, womanlike, where she had not thought of other women in connection with him, they suddenly became a challenge. Even the intrusion of Nurse Drake upset the balance and magnified his importance.

When the salmon was served, he poured out her wine and stooped to kiss the top of her head. She stared up at him, and their eyes met in an expression which made no attempt to conceal their desire.

'You look beautiful in the candlelight,' he murmured.

His nearness was electrifying; she wanted to lift her face to his and feel his kiss, but managed to change the mood and quote lightly, 'As Noel Coward said, "Moonlight can be cruelly deceptive!"'

'Not when you are just as beautiful in the sunlight,' he insisted as he sat down beside her, pouring out his own wine and raising his glass. 'To us.'

They drank, their gaze holding, the deep silence full of promise, and when the meal was over and they returned to the sitting room, it was like a drama building up to an inevitable climax.

'*Andrea?*' he said hoarsely and in an unspoken question.

She stretched out her hand, which he clasped almost painfully, and slowly, deliberately, they moved towards the bedroom.

He took her in his arms, at first gently and then with mounting passion; they undressed with a naturalness that made time irrelevant, and sank into the softness of the bed. His kiss awakened a deep inward rapture while their bodies touched, pressing closer in urgent desire until that moment of possession and the final cry of fulfilment.

'Darling!' he whispered, his lips against her neck.

Andrea gave a little shiver of happiness when finally they moved and lay side by side, his arm round her shoulder, his hand cupping her breast, his lips on her forehead.

'I can't quite believe this is happening: that I'm here with you,' he said, drawing her closer.

Andrea was conscious of a strange inevitability, and cried involuntarily, 'Let's enjoy the days, Garth, and not try to analyse them out of existence. It is enough that we are together in understanding.'

He looked down wonderingly. The possibility of making love to her had obsessed him since he returned from holiday.

'Is that really what you want?' he asked quietly.

She gave a little contented sigh. 'Yes, I want to guard this happiness, this freedom.' She looked deeply into his eyes. 'I always hoped it would be like this,' she added honestly and without reserve.

'With *me*?' His voice was low.

'You took shape out of a phantom figure,' she admitted. 'Then, suddenly after you'd been away, I knew, even if I wouldn't admit it, that I wanted this to happen.'

Passion stirred between them and his lips parted hers, his arms tightened round her. A little later they slept, oblivious of time or the world.

Andrea arrived at Clee View earlier than usual the following morning, willing herself into a professional mood while memories of the previous night surged back to cloud her judgment and re-awaken ecstasy. It had been midnight when Garth left her, and she hoped to have a few minutes alone with him before the staff arrived, but Elaine greeted her brightly as she opened the door.

'Two early birds,' she said. 'I'm afraid I interrupted Dr Howard's breakfast, but there was a question I wanted to ask him, and . . .'

Garth, hearing what had been said as he came out of the dining room, glanced at Andrea and said, 'Good morning.' He added, 'I'd like a word with you before we begin surgery.'

Elaine hovered, and then disappeared.

Andrea and Garth walked together into his consulting room. Their eyes met, the gaze deepening as his arms went round her, each remembering, their silence significant.

'And now, Dr Howard,' Andrea said smoothly, 'this is where we change channels and concentrate on work!'

He stood there, a challenge to her resolve as he kissed her very swiftly, before agreeing.

'I'm attending the Spicer case this morning,' he said gravely.

'Lung.'

'Yes; we can't tell how far it has spread.'

Andrea moved her hands in a little despairing gesture and said angrily, 'We can raise millions for everything and everyone, but so little to try to cure cancer! Our hospitals are crying out for equipment . . .' She stopped. 'Mustn't get on my hobby-horse!'

'I love you on your hobby-horse!' he exclaimed, and hurried on, 'You're having dinner with Douglas?' He spoke tentatively.

'Yes. And, Garth? While we're together, I shall never . . .'

She didn't need to finish the sentence, because he broke in, 'Nor I, Andrea.'

It was as though a satisfactory chapter had been written in an unfinished book.

'Nurse Drake was here early,' Andrea commented a few seconds later.

'She's very keen to excel at her job.' Garth moved to his desk.

'I'd better have a word with Mrs Boyer, and see what the day's going to be like.'

Their eyes met. They might have been in each other's arms.

The last surgery patient came into Andrea's room looking worried and nervous. She was thirty-five, slim, attractive; married, with a son and daughter of ten and twelve respectively.

'Well, Mrs Madison, what seems to be wrong?' Andrea smiled, and indicated the patients' chair. She liked Mrs Madison, whose dark hair cascaded, shoulder-length, in natural waves, making her look younger than her years. Andrea noticed the worried frown between her brows and the rather awkward manner in which she moved her shoulders.

'Actually, it's my breasts—the right one in particular. I've lumps in them.'

'Lumps!' Andrea echoed, feeling slightly dismayed, but a little consoled by the plural.

'They are so painful and swollen that I can hardly bear my bra. They're far more tender than they were before I had the children.'

'How long has this been going on?' Andrea saw from her notes that Mrs Madison hadn't consulted her for six months. She had also been sterilised with the birth of the second child, so pregnancy could not be a cause of the symptom.

'Since February. I've always had pre-menstrual tenderness, but nothing like this . . . Oh, Dr Forbes, I'm terrified!' The words rushed out.

'I doubt very much if you've any cause to be,' said Andrea, 'but let's examine you.'

The breasts were enlarged, tender and lumpy.

'They swell before your period starts, and go down once it has started? I can tell that they are extremely painful.'

Mrs Madison nodded, looking anxiously into Andrea's eyes.

'You have mastitis—nodular mastitis,' Andrea told her. 'A hormonal imbalance . . . When is your period due?'

'In about eight days.'

'So they're at their worst at the moment.'

'Yes.' There was a moment of awkward silence. 'It

isn't just putting up with the—the pain, but I can't bear my husband to touch me. It lasts so *long*, too. I'm sometimes like this for over two weeks at a time. It isn't anything I can hide, or bear without . . .'

Andrea said, 'I understand. Actually, if you'd been thrashed, you would not be in much more pain and discomfort than you are now!'

'Is there anything I can have, or do?' It was an urgent plea.

'I'm going to prescribe you some capsules—specifically for breast disorders. And I shall want to see you next week.'

Mrs Madison relaxed and smiled. 'I've been afraid to come to you, in case . . . But'—faint colour stole into her cheeks—'since it is affecting our love-making, well . . .' She hurried on, a little shyly, 'We've always had a wonderful life, and I saw it all being ruined for both of us.'

Andrea, despite her professional concentration, could not help thinking that yesterday she would not have understood what the ramifications were, except by implication. Now she understood, and the image of Garth was suddenly visual. She wrote out the prescription and handed it to Mrs Madison.

'I've given you a small dose . . . Let's hope this will solve your problem,' she said with a gentle smile. 'How is the family?'

'Fine . . . Duncan (her husband) is now with the Horton Group and still passing exams in engineering! Andrew and Una are as exhausting as children can be, and mad on computers!'

Andrea indicated her interest, and then said, 'Make sure that you wear the right size bra.'

'I've several sizes, because I can hardly bear them to

touch me, but I must have the support.'

'Support is essential,' Andrea commented.

'And I don't want to lose my figure,' came the swift response.

Andrea smiled. 'And make an appointment for next week,' she reminded her.

'I will. Thank you, Dr Forbes.'

Andrea relaxed after the door shut, feeling a wave of happiness and satisfaction.

Garth appeared. 'Time for a coffee? Routine cases this morning, so I've finished surgery.'

'So have I.' She switched down the intercom and spoke to Clare. Could they have two coffees?

Clare grinned as she took the message and looked at Mrs Boyer and Elaine, who had just joined them. 'It may be my imagination, but haven't Dr Howard and Dr Forbes been more matey since he got back from his holidays?'

Mrs Boyer echoed the word, 'matey', with disdain. 'Really, Clare! You do use the most extraordinary language.'

'All the same, you know what I mean. If you haven't noticed, you must be blind.' She looked at Elaine, who had stiffened. 'What do you think?'

'Since I've been here only a short time, and not before Dr Howard went away,' she replied discreetly, 'I am in no position to judge.' She added to Mrs Boyer's delight, 'And I don't think it is any business of ours!'

Clare decided that there was something just a little too perfect about Nurse Drake.

When the coffee was made, Elaine said, lifting the tray from the table, 'I'll take this in. I want a word with Dr Howard, and I saw him go into Dr Forbes's room.'

As she disappeared from view, disappointed, Clare

exploded, 'Eyes in the back of her ruddy head!' She stared Mrs Boyer out, and there was silence.

Andrea saw the nurse with surprise, but Elaine explained, 'I thought this was a good opportunity to have a word with you both.' She put the tray down and handed Andrea her cup, and then Garth. 'It seems I've been here for years!' she said. 'Surgery went smoothly, I thought . . . I had one amusing patient who complained of a chilblain when in fact she'd broken her toe! It was swollen, all colours of the rainbow, and painful. She seemed quite cheerful when I told her what had happened, and that it would find a place for itself and nothing could really be done.' She went on confidently, 'People are amazing, especially in casualty, but one has more time here and it can be most amusing . . . You know a Mrs Lacey, Dr Howard? . . . I've made an appointment for you to see her tomorrow; she has a nasty cough and, as you know, suffers from bronchitis.' She added critically, 'And smokes.'

Garth said indulgently, 'I've known Mrs Lacey ever since I've been here, Nurse. Why didn't you send her in?'

'It would have upset your schedule and you wouldn't be drinking your coffee now, if I had,' Elaine said, feeling that she had shown discretion and consideration.

'She has quite a long way to come,' Garth said with feeling. 'In future, I *always* wish to see Mrs Lacey.'

Elaine resented her position. 'I don't understand people who smoke when they have chest complaints,' she said severely.

Andrea watched apprehensively as the tension built up, and Garth said, 'Mrs Lacey is a widow who lives alone; she smokes two cigarettes on a Sunday as a little treat. It isn't always the best thing to prolong life at the expense of happiness. One has to strike a balance. It might be highly beneficial if smoking and drinking were banned altogether, but it would be a pretty dull existence.'

'You don't smoke!' The words came out instinctively, and she added hurriedly, 'That was the first thing I noticed.'

Andrea said with authority, changing the trend of the conversation, 'And if Dr Howard should not be available, I will always fit Mrs Lacey in. She's a valued loyal patient.' Andrea paused. 'There were no other problems, I take it?'

'None. I passed on the doubtful cases.'

'Thank you, Nurse.' Garth's voice had a note of dismissal in it.

Elaine left them. She knew she had been too dogmatic and not made a good impression.

'She'd be a tartar as a Sister,' Andrea said involuntarily, watching Garth carefully.

'She'll never be a Sister *here*,' he said almost harshly, and then went on cautiously, 'But she's new and overanxious, so let's not be too hard. So far she's certainly saved us a lot of donkey-work, and she is a pretty good judge.'

'You're a very fair man,' said Andrea.

'Hell can be made up of sitting in both chairs!' he retorted.

Andrea hated to admit that she wished she had never seen, or heard of, Nurse Drake, and that she had an uneasy feeling about her generally. The bold familiarity of her words, *'You don't smoke'*, left the impression of someone determined to make her influence felt, and even her authority established.

'Which sounds,' Andrea said with sudden concern, 'as

though you've had experience in that direction.'

'Just a poor way of admitting to the weakness, if you like, of seeing both points of view . . . And I wanted our coffee to be drunk in peace!' He looked solemn. 'Now I must get to the Spicer case. Shall I see you again today?'

The thought of Douglas lay between them.

'Impossible to say. I've visits and appointments here later.'

'You're not good for my concentration,' he confessed.

'That makes two of us! We shall have to see.'

'No emotional involvement,' he quoted reflectively, went over to her desk, kissed her with a lingering passion, and left.

Andrea sat there, heart racing. She realised suddenly that she was not on surgery that evening, in which case Garth would be taking it, this time with Nurse Drake. An unfamiliar spike of apprehension, even jealousy, touched her.

Elaine waylaid Garth on his way out. 'I'm afraid I was a bit dogmatic just now.' She looked up at him with a wheedling apology. 'But it isn't easy to behave as though you were a stranger.'

His voice was firm. 'You created this situation, but I will not have any friction. Neither are you to usurp my authority or that of Dr Forbes.'

Elaine spat out, 'You think a lot of her, don't you?'

'She would not be my partner otherwise. Now, I must hurry, and I don't want any more of this kind of thing.'

'Garth?'

But he took no notice as he got into his car and was lost in the traffic. She turned back into the house, coming face to face with Andrea.

'I was just having a word with Dr Howard. He's a very understanding man, isn't he?'

What, Andrea asked herself, would necessitate Nurse Drake following Garth out of the house and to his car?

'About a problem?' she asked.

'Just a personal query . . . Has Clare told you that Dr Jayson called and asked if you'd ring him back?'

'Yes.' She wanted to suggest that Clare was perfectly capable of relaying a message.

'Such an amusing girl. I don't pretend to understand her outlook.'

Andrea smiled, looked Elaine in the eye and said, 'Naturally; you're almost a different generation.'

Elaine winced.

Andrea walked along the corridor as she said, 'Clare is wonderful with the patients, young or old. They love her. Manner is everything, particularly in a small practice.' She paused at her consulting-room door, 'Or for that matter, any practice.'

Elaine bit her lip. The charming Dr Forbes didn't miss a trick!

When Andrea spoke to Douglas, all he wanted was to pick her up a little later than previously arranged.

'Why not let me meet you at the Feathers? Save time, and I'm quite at home there,' she suggested.

It was arranged.

Andrea did her visits, delighted that Donald Maddox had proved her diagnosis by his recovery, and that for the moment she was free from particularly worrying cases, so that when she returned to Clee View (having had coffee and a sandwich at the Lodge Buttery near the Castle, to spare herself the chore of getting it for herself), she was ready for the afternoon patients. Mrs Boyer and Clare were on their own; Nurse Drake was at lunch. Andrea despised herself for inwardly sympathising with them because they appeared to be showing all the relaxation of pupils when the teacher was away.

'Coffee, Dr Forbes?' Clare said eagerly, enjoying the moments—rare enough—when Andrea was free and able to exchange a few words.

'Just had one,' Andrea said, thanking her for the offer. 'I sneaked into the Lodge Buttery to avoid the bother of making my own sandwich!'

'We could always get you sandwiches,' said Clare.

Andrea's smile embraced them both. 'Haven't you enough to do? I'm just lazy.'

Even Mrs Boyer scoffed. 'If you're lazy, then I never get out of bed!'

They laughed together.

Clare said smoothly, 'Dr Howard's back, and, to use his own words, "grabbing some lunch".'

Andrea nodded and exclaimed, 'Which will surprise his stomach! How did he look?'

Mrs Boyer and Clare exchanged glances.

'Down,' Clare replied.

'I'll have a word with him.' Andrea gave them an understanding look as she left.

'She's a super person,' Clare said affectionately.

Garth had pushed away his half-eaten meal and was looking at a newspaper which he was not reading. His face lit up as Andrea came into the dining room and sat down at the table.

She said, 'How did it go?'

'He's lost a lung, and we're doing a biopsy on the other one, which is suspect.' He shook his head. 'He's forty, Andrea, and now I've got to see his wife. God, how I dread that! They've two sons, one at boarding school and the other nearly old enough to go. They manage by making sacrifices.'

'People can live with half of one lung.' Andrea spoke gently.

'I know. I also know the suffering in between. The bare facts never state the case, do they?' He went on, 'This is "nothing"; the other is "simple"; that is "curable". Nicely packaged into neat words, but not taking into account the domestic upheaval, the suffering of those *waiting*——'

Andrea stretched out her hand and clasped his.

'I know,' she said. 'I know.' Her sigh was deep. 'Maybe we ought not to have been doctors.'

He shook his head. 'At least we can be of some help to the relatives by understanding their problems.'

'And *explaining*,' Andrea added. 'That's so important.'

They looked at each other and nodded.

Andrea said suddenly, 'I think I'll look in on Mrs Lacey before I start the afternoon appointments. We don't want her getting bronchitis, and she never comes to "be a nuisance", as she calls it.'

'Would you?' He sounded relieved, then his voice was hard. 'Nurse Drake won't do *that* again.'

'I feel I've blundered over her,' said Andrea.

'Nonsense; we've been into that. She'll adapt to our ways. She knows she has to.'

'Reminds me of someone I once knew who always used to say that there is such a thing as being too right, and too efficient. Human problems need resilience.'

Garth stared straight ahead of him. He agreed, but didn't enlarge on the matter. They got up from the table, arms touching, eyes meeting. Emotion flared as memories of the previous night held them. They both knew that any demonstration would be fatal, as they hurried away to their respective rooms.

Andrea arrived at the Feathers a matter of minutes after the appointed time. The hotel, built in 1603, was the most famous timber-framed building in the town. She went through into the small, attractive bar, where a fifteenth-century tapestry of 'Le Pressoir' (wine-making) hung over the fireplace. A large sideboard displayed brass and a copper kettle, and an oak settle completed a picture of comfortable antiquity.

Douglas joined her within seconds.

Andrea saw him through new eyes as a result of her relationship with Garth, who had sharpened her sexual consciousness, and she studied him intently as they sipped their dry sherries. He was tall, lean, with slightly rugged features, level brows and a direct gaze which could be disarming. He didn't use two words where one would do, and was the foremost gynaecologist in Ludlow. His and Andrea's friendship had begun desultorily when she joined Garth's practice, and deepened with time; their meetings were sporadic, but never a matter of casual acceptance.

'You look extremely happy.' His blue eyes met hers and he threaded a hand through his light brown hair because a stray lock had a habit of falling over his forehead.

'Shouldn't I be?'

'I hoped you might have missed me.'

'I *wondered*,' she commented evasively, and remembered Garth's words that Douglas was in love with her. She had never given the matter any serious thought until now, her perception intensified by recent experience.

'That's something,' he said ruefully, introducing a note that contrasted with their previous light-hearted acceptance of friendship. 'Shall we eat? I'm starving! My diet of black coffee doesn't seem to have been very sustaining today.'

They went into the dining room, where wine racks were stacked in an inglenook and against a natural stone wall. Pewter platters stood on the chimneybreast. The carpet was a mixture of lilac, purple and pink, and the tablecloths and napkins were pink, with carnations to complete the décor. They were at home there, and went to a corner table at which they had dined many times. They chose chicken simmered in orange and walnut sauce and, to start, melon. The thought of Garth overwhelmed her. Her being there with Douglas seemed a strange juxtaposition after the previous evening.

'I hear you've got a nurse to help you out,' Douglas remarked, having chosen the wine. 'Garth had mentioned it vaguely, and so had you, but I somehow didn't see it coming off.'

'Pressure of work,' she said quickly.

'And reluctance to get another partner. I'm damned near that position myself . . . Keeping up with patients is one thing; with technology, another. These days there is precious little breathing space.'

Andrea relaxed. It was quite absurd, but she would like to tell Douglas about Garth; it seemed almost a betrayal of their friendship not to do so, yet, she argued, there was no reason whatever for the confidence. It was just that Douglas's attitude suggested a greater involvement than on previous occasions, bringing an element of suspense, even of tension, in the sudden and unusual silences.

'We've found a highly efficient nurse,' said Andrea.

'Good! I'm a contradiction,' he countered with a little chuckle. 'I've great respect for "highly efficient women", but don't particularly like them.'

'Chauvinist! You want your slippers warming beside the fire!'

'But *not* the "little woman" to go with them. I'm sure you know what I mean,' he added.

'Oh, I do know,' she agreed. 'You just want the best of both worlds!'

'And that's where you've spoilt me for other women,' he told her feelingly.

'I?' She gave a little gasp.

'Yes. You're a clever doctor, a wonderful emergency person, and yet sufficiently feminine to inspire the belief that help would not be rejected.'

Andrea laughed to hide her embarrassment and apprehension. 'It must be the wine,' she teased.

He held her gaze very earnestly. 'No, it isn't the wine, Andrea. It's because I'm in love with you. Will you marry me?'

And even as Douglas spoke, Elaine was ringing Garth, her voice low and appealing as she said, 'Can I see you—come over to Clee View now? I need your guidance.' She paused effectively. 'For old times' sake,' she added in a whisper. 'Yes, I'll be with you in a few minutes.'

CHAPTER FOUR

DOUGLAS'S words, 'Will you marry me?', plunged Andrea into the world of reality. The question was direct and inescapable. She looked astounded.

'You must have been blind or naïve, or both, not to have realised,' he said after a moment of silence.

Andrea looked at him a little helplessly. 'I don't go about imagining that men are in love with me!'

'I'm not "men",' he retorted. 'Because I haven't suggested our leaping into bed, that doesn't mean that the thought hasn't been in my mind!'

Andrea smiled. 'I love your friendship,' she said frankly, 'but I'm not in love with you. I often wonder if I shall ever be in love. Flirtations, sexual excitement——' She stopped. How would she be able to describe her relationship with Garth, even if she wished?

'We could perhaps have all that, and marriage. A natural progression on your part.' He looked at her intently. 'I'm a reasonably civilised sort of chap, and I'd give you breathing space.'

'If I married you, I shouldn't need it,' she said. 'I don't want to marry anyone, Douglas.'

He sighed, sipped his wine and looked disappointed, then a little complacent.

'You will,' he said with confidence. 'All this modern "live-in girl-friends"; "marriage will ruin our relationship"; "single-parent families are better than two"— fine! I sometimes think that our generation refuses to face up to the fact that we grow old, and then a little old-fashioned normality would be comforting to go with the wrinkles!'

'That still gives me years of freedom,' Andrea quipped.

'Then I'll stick it out,' he said blandly.

They laughed together, and she had never liked him better.

Meanwhile, at Clee View, Garth said, 'I fail to see why it is necessary for you to come here to discuss any problem with me, Elaine.'

'There's never any time to talk to you alone during working hours . . . It's about a house. There's one about to come on the market just off the High Street. I wondered if you'd look at it with me. I have an order to view a week today—Wednesday.'

'You'll have your surveyor and go through the usual procedures. It has absolutely nothing to do with me,' he said firmly. 'I can't stop you buying a house here, but I do not have to be involved with it. In fact I would suggest that you cut out altogether the idea of settling in this area. You haven't made a particularly auspicious start in the practice, and have adopted an autocratic attitude generally, which has alienated both Mrs Boyer and Clare.'

'*And* Dr Forbes,' Elaine stated. 'That's what you really mean, isn't it?'

'Dr Forbes can speak for herself,' he said, 'and has a good deal of influence.'

'I don't need reminding of *that* . . . Oh, Garth, can't you see how difficult this is for me?' She looked forlorn and appealing. 'Nothing has gone right in my life, and losing my husband was the last blow. I want to put down some roots here——'

'Then you've gone about it in quite the wrong way. I

don't for the life of me see why you chose to come here, to me, in the first place.'

'Probably,' she said after a long pause, 'because I realise what you mean to me.'

He stiffened. 'Don't introduce that note, or I won't agree to your staying here. For my part, I'd prefer the past were out in the open, and . . . '

'No!' she said with a harsh fear. 'You gave me your word.'

He sighed and shrugged his shoulders.

She changed her attitude, looking at him with a pleading gentleness. 'Christopher would want us to be friends,' she said with telling emphasis. 'Or have you forgotten?'

There was a heavy silence before he replied, 'You know the answer to that.'

'Very well, then . . . come to see the house. *Please* help me, Garth? I've no one else to turn to now. And I'll win Mrs Boyer and Clare over, to say nothing of Dr Forbes. I've just been disorientated in adapting to strange and unusual circumstances, after all.'

'You are responsible for those circumstances,' he reminded her without sympathy.

'I know. I've behaved foolishly . . . But now, if everything goes well, can we be friends?'

'That's up to you. I won't have any trouble in this practice, Elaine, and I should have no compunction about asking you to leave. Remember that,' he said firmly. 'What is more, I've no intention of repeating this warning.'

'You've been very patient with me, Garth,' she said softly, and her dark eyes met his with open admiration. 'You will come to see the house with me? It isn't just agents' talk that it will be snapped up quickly.'

Garth felt awkward. He didn't want to tell Andrea of the mission; equally, he had no wish to keep it from her. It was, after all, he argued, a reasonable request, even though Elaine was supposed to be a stranger. Her position merited a little indulgence, since she was on her own and new to the town. He was satisfied that she would alter her tactics and fit harmoniously into the scheme of things from then on.

Elaine was all smiles the following morning, toning down her voice, asking Mrs Boyer for guidance, and even laughing with Clare over some trivial happening. She had no illusions. Garth would make no bones about sacking her, and that was the last thing she wanted. She had played her cards badly thus far, giving way to a natural jealousy and an inability to adjust to circumstances.

She waited until Andrea joined them in Mrs Boyer's office before she said, 'I wonder if we can arrange things next Wednesday so that I have my lunch hour from twelve o'clock? I have a house to look at, and Dr Howard has kindly offered to give me his advice about it. He can get away then . . . Would you mind changing your time, Clare?'

Clare, open-mouthed, stammered, 'Why, no!'

Dr *Howard* going to see a house with her!

Andrea struggled to conceal her surprise as she went along to Garth's consulting room. Why on earth should Garth want to become involved with Elaine's house purchase, particularly after all that had been said? There was something that didn't ring true, and she mentioned the fact to him without concealing her disapproval.

'I was obviously going to tell you,' he said without prevarication, aware how odd it must look to Andrea, and that he had not given due consideration to the matter. He refused to admit to himself that he had, when it came to it, been persuaded, rather like someone who had wielded the big stick and wished to atone for the harshness. Looking a little awkward, he hurried on, 'Nurse Drake telephoned me last evening and came along wishing to have my advice. As she knows nothing about property——'

'You don't have to *explain* to me. If you want to help her, it is your business.'

'I was very blunt with her,' Garth hastened on, 'and warned her that I should have no remorse about sacking her unless she changed her attitude. She was very apologetic . . . All the same, I should have refused to be drawn into her affairs.'

Andrea stared him out.

'It's rather ironical that you were insistent that we should avoid social contact.' There was trace of cynicism in her voice. 'Obviously that no longer applies.'

'On the contrary: this is purely advice on a business matter,' he stressed again. 'I quite appreciate that it was a mistake.'

Andrea was aware that Elaine's timing had been perfect. A shiver went over her as she fought fear and jealousy, hating the sickening effect of both and vowing to overcome them. Why build up a trivial incident? It suddenly made her feel small.

It was not until the following Wednesday morning that Garth said somewhat challengingly and belligerently, 'You haven't told me anything about your evening with Douglas.'

'You didn't ask me! He wants to marry me. I said, "No."'

Emotion flared between them. They exchanged stormy looks, and then moved swiftly into each other's arms, passion all the greater because of the momentary disharmony. A second or two later he released her, their gaze deep and significant.

Then he asked solemnly, 'Have you seen the local paper this morning?'

Immediately she exclaimed in a breath, '*Stephanie!* I shall never forget that inquest, or the fact that I had to admit that I'd seen her shortly before she died.' Andrea's face clouded, apprehension darkening her eyes. 'Have they built it up?'

He handed her the newspaper, indicating the item which read:

> A verdict of misadventure was returned on the death of Miss Stephanie Landon, aged fifteen, who was found drowned in the swimming pool of her parents' home. The post mortem revealed that Miss Landon was ten weeks pregnant.

'No sensationalism, at least,' Andrea said with a sigh. 'And Myrna Landon lied and pleaded ignorance of it all.'

'That kept the boy's name out of it,' Garth said. 'Not that there was any charity in her motive.'

'She will never visit me again,' Andrea said.

Elaine came into the room at that moment, pleasantly business-like. 'Clare wants to know if either of you can see Mrs Gordon before surgery starts. Transport is very restricted for her.'

'Of course: I'll see her, Nurse,' Garth said immediately. 'Oh, and I'd like you to be here while I examine Mrs Burke.'

'Yes, Dr Howard.' She stood aside to allow Andrea to pass her, and then shut Garth's door.

Andrea's first patient was well known to her—

Maureen Carey, married to a rich industrialist; a little Napoleon to whom she was devoted. She was expecting her fourth child, having had three daughters in quick succession.

'Neville is getting obsessional about its being a boy,' she said, her grey eyes full of anxiety and pain. She looked at Andrea, with whom she had been friendly for the past year. 'Oh, Andrea, the suspense of it all is driving me mad!'

Andrea disliked Neville intensely; he represented everything she scorned in a man. Neither his success, nor his money, impressed her. His charm was false, which irritated her because, through it, he assumed that all women were ready to obey his every command.

Andrea said stoutly, 'It is the man who determines the sex of the child, and if he won't accept that, he is betraying abysmal ignorance.' She studied Maureen with professional concern. 'It will not help if you are going through this pregnancy in a state of worry and fear.'

Maureen exclaimed despairingly, 'He says this is my last chance! He'll leave me and marry someone else, in the hope of having a son to carry on the name and take over all his business interests. He's mentioned divorce several times lately, and knows I should never stand in the way of his getting one,' she added abjectly. Then she rushed on, 'I'm here because I want you to arrange for me to have a scan, or whatever it is, so that I can know the sex of the child. At least I'd be spared the suspense.'

Andrea sighed, and shook her head firmly. 'An ultrasound scan won't tell you the sex before the twenty-sixth week.'

'Oh!'

'And if it could, and it was proved to be a girl, how

would you face up to the remaining weeks? I'd like to have a word with Neville. He hasn't much respect for women in any position of authority, but I might make him see sense.'

Maureen burst into tears. It was the first time Andrea had seen her cry, for she was a strong character until it came to her love for Neville, which seemed to rob her of all strength and confidence, so that she was rather like a rabbit with a stoat.

'I'm so sorry,' she whispered. 'I hate a crying woman, but, somehow, it all seems so hopeless. I wanted two children, but not this production-line method. Have you ever had any other case like mine?' She drew in her breath sharply and the tears dried up.

'Oh yes,' Andrea said regretfully. 'There's no unique case. Every one is duplicated at some time or another. We only *think* that our situation is different.'

'I wish Neville didn't make me feel so *ill*. He's so cutting, hurtful, and I don't seem to be able to take it any more.'

Andrea studied the pale face, knowing that, physically, Maureen was a very healthy woman whose pregnancy was normal. She took her blood pressure which was up a little, as expected; insisted that she rest, and said finally, 'I shall have a word with Neville. Meanwhile, don't argue with him. Is he at his Ludlow office, by the way?'

'Yes, just for a few days. Then he goes to some unpronounceable place in the Middle East for ten days. He seems to be involved in everything.' There was a little apologetic pause before Maureen added, 'I'm sorry to have burdened you with all this, but I'd reached the screeching point of a whistling kettle . . . Will you really have a word with him?'

'I most certainly will.'

And Andrea did; arriving at Neville Carey's office, having made sure he was in; demanding to see him when told that he was not available, and more or less thrusting her way into his sanctum with its brown studded leather chairs and large mahogany desk which gave an air of opulence. Andrea marvelled anew at Maureen's devotion to him. He was a short thick-set man whose thin face did not conform to his stature. But he was impeccably dressed, brisk, and oozed success. Only the best was good enough for Neville Carey who had fought his way up and used every skill to attain his present position.

'Andrea?' he said in surprise, but on a note of suspicion, as he dismissed the apologetic clerk with a wave of the hand.

'I've just seen Maureen,' she said directly.

'I've nothing to say to you so far as she is concerned, so don't waste your time, or mine.' His beady eyes narrowed. 'I'm determined to have a son, and if she can't give me one . . .'

Andrea looked at him with a withering contempt that made his eyebrows shoot up and his face darken in anger.

'You're a bully, Neville, because, despite your bombast, you're basically insecure. You want a son to reinforce your security, believing that he will perpetuate your success. It's unthinkable, isn't it, that he might be a drop-out who would loathe your business life?'

'I—I——' he spluttered.

Andrea went on, 'You have health, a lovely, and loving, wife and three intelligent normal children, and if you cause Maureen any further distress and unhappiness, you'll have me to deal with. At this moment, you're endangering her health!'

'No one dares to speak to me like this!' he thundered.

'I dare, because your behaviour makes you a very small, insignificant man. You want the star on the top of the Christmas tree, and if you can't have it, you'll make life hell for those around you. Remember one thing: you might marry two or three times and still produce only daughters; whereas Maureen might marry again once, and have a son. Think about that sometime—and grow up.' She flung at him as she went towards the door, 'But, remember, I hold a watching brief.'

He stood there shocked, staggered and speechless.

She felt better as she went out into the sunlit day. But the shadow at the back of her mind clouded her vision a few minutes later, as she thought of Garth with Nurse Drake, looking over her possible future home.

Elaine fell in love with the house, which was renovated seventeenth century, and a mixture of old and new, the kitchen and bathroom units impeccable.

'Isn't it rather large?' Garth noted the four bedrooms and three reception rooms.

'I have my furniture in store—more than enough for here.' She added, 'I don't like small houses, and it would be a saleable property in the event of my plans changing.' She looked up at him. 'I might, also, marry again . . .'

Garth's spirits lifted. 'Which is more than likely,' he said in a tone which she found flattering.

'Meanwhile, property is always a good investment,' she said practically. 'What do you think?'

'That the upkeep would be considerable, and if you married again, your future husband would most probably have his own home.'

'Meaning that he would not be prepared to do the moving?' She looked innocent.

'This is all purely hypothetical,' he said, a little unnerved by her steady gaze.

'But you have a point,' she agreed. 'And the upkeep *would* be expensive. I have one smaller property——'

'I can't possibly spare any more time,' Garth said immediately. 'When you've found something that seems to be more suitable, I'll willingly have a look at it.'

Elaine fell in with the suggestion, having known that this particular house was far too large. But it had already served her purpose. Garth was there, beside her. The ice had been broken.

'I'll look around,' she said. 'One always panics when told that another buyer is in the offing! Human nature to want that which may be out of reach . . . Thank you for coming, Garth. You've saved me from plunging into folly. It is too large, and the problem of the domestic work . . . But it's a most attractive place.'

'I agree there.' He looked at his watch.

She didn't hesitate then to say tactfully, 'We must get back. I'm afraid I've wasted your lunch hour.'

His smile was wry. 'Since you know what that signifies, I don't think it matters.'

'Yes,' she laughed. 'The words are misnomers. A doctor's lunch hour is very elastic.' She walked quickly to the front door and handed him the keys with a little intimate gesture. 'Make sure we've locked up properly. I'm not much good at it.'

Garth looked down at her. In his thankfulness to be spared any hassle, she seemed charming and without threat to the future.

During the weeks that followed, late spring merged into summer and harvest time, when the rolling acres of Shropshire lay golden beneath clear blue skies, like some vast estate magnificently tended by its owner, with Ludlow the jewel in the crown, its planned streets and old buildings mellow in the changing light, the magnificent church, dedicated to St Laurence, etched against sunset and dawn and dominating the scene by day.

Elaine eventually found a small house near King Street, where the shops still retained windows with small panes of glass. She furnished it artistically, with the antiques she and Ralph—her late husband—had chosen together. Her attitude couldn't have been faulted, and she won herself a place in the practice which endeared her to staff and patients alike, joking about the 'horror' she had been on first taking over her job. It wouldn't have been true to say that she and Andrea had become intimate friends, but they were sufficiently in harmony to have an occasional meal or drink together.

Her relationship with Garth was more difficult to determine, but Andrea told herself that it was an excellent example of an amicable business-like association, lightened by a touch of humour to take the edge off formality. Elaine had craved the favour of being called by her Christian name out of professional hours, and the effect had been relaxing. But while Andrea had accepted the pattern, thankful that the association had turned out so well, she still had a strange foreboding when tension mounted, and she could not rid herself of a faint jealousy which she decried, and curbed on every occasion. There was just something about Elaine's behaviour with Garth that often struck a false note. From her own point of view, Andrea could not fault him during those months; he had accepted their life on her terms, but recently she had become restless, with a feeling that, in some way, life was inadequate and without any goal. And on this particular evening she found herself watching Garth, realising that he looked strained and uncomfortable.

It was early September, and Garth had suggested that they go out to a restaurant near Leominster, eleven miles away; but Andrea retreated—she wanted to be alone, to catch up on neglected tasks and, in effect, take stock. She explained as tactfully as she could, and he drew her gaze to his with an unnerving intensity.

'You don't have to make excuses to avoid being with me.' His voice was cold, his expression forbidding.

She was shocked, lost to his attitude while concentrating on her own, and she hadn't any valid excuse, which distressed her.

'And if you prefer Douglas's company,' he rushed on, sparing her a reply, 'say so.'

It was their first confrontation, and they faced each other with all the passion and pain of disharmony.

'This is ridiculous!' she cried. 'Why bring Douglas into it?'

'Because he is in it, and I've noticed a change in you just recently.'

The words were like a hammer-blow, stunning, leaving her distressed, awkward and immediately fearful. She and Garth could not *quarrel*! It was unthinkable; and about what?

'"Change"?' she echoed fearfully.

'You might have gone off into another world . . . I've respected your not wanting any emotional involvement, but you hardly seem satisfied with life at the moment.' He added, his voice sharp, 'Neither am I.'

Immediately she panicked. It was one thing for her to be restless, but a vastly different matter when it came to him. But she dared not give vent to her feelings or she would have been in his arms at that moment, passion wiping out reality.

'I'm sorry,' she said stiffly. 'I think we'll both make more sense tomorrow.'

'Silence won't solve anything,' he growled.

She made a desperate effort. 'There's nothing to solve . . . All this because I didn't . . .'

He cut in, 'You didn't *want* to come out with me this evening. Let's not evade the issue. But you know that it goes far deeper than that triviality, Andrea.'

She felt that she had suddenly got into quicksands that were sucking her down to suffocation point. She knew, too, that she had fallen in love with him and was no longer content with their present relationship.

CHAPTER FIVE

ANDREA heard Garth's cold voice with a sense of shock, and was dragged back from the precipice of discovery into a world which he dominated. The previous easy attraction, sexually expressed, gave way to a tense aching love, new and even frightening. *'No emotional involvement'*, she had stipulated, which made her seem foolish, almost naïve. How could a woman possibly accept Garth merely as a lover without any deeper ties other than a professional friendship that never intruded? So this was love: this overwhelming need, this fierce longing for more that sensual satisfaction.

His eyes looked into hers, not with desire or gentleness, but with the fury of baffled anger, so that her only weapon was attack.

'Don't turn this into a drama,' she managed to say.

He stared at her aghast. 'The cliché, that I don't understand you, is all I can think of to say!' he exclaimed. 'You seem to have changed as you stand there —remote, retreating from me in some inexplicable way.'

Her shoulders drooped and then squared as she drew on courage and dignity. She must adjust to the changed situation and her own limitations.

'Just because I wanted an evening on my own!' she challenged.

'That is an over-simplification, and you know it. It is your general attitude.'

'My "attitude", as you call it, merely seeks reciprocal understanding.'

He made a hopeless gesture. 'I've never seen you in this mood.'

She wished she could tell him that she had never before felt in this mood, and that the realisation of her love for him had struck like an earthquake. She ought, she argued self-critically, to have allowed for its inevitability. How easy it was to believe one could play chess with human emotions, and how terrifying to find that no matter what moves one contrived, nature would always win the game.

She couldn't fight him any more, and fell back on a quiet shaken plea as she said, 'Please Garth, don't let's argue.'

'"Argue"!' It was an explosive echo. 'You have a curious way of twisting words. Anyway, we'll leave it . . . I shan't get a straight answer to a straight question, so what is the use of my wasting my breath?'

She averted her eyes and made no response, just watched him as he strode to the door and, without another word, left. The silence of his consulting room, and the house in general, made it seem like a tomb in which she had been buried. The lengthening shadows of late September crept stealthily across his desk . . . Why hadn't she agreed to have dinner with him? Why retreat at the first note of danger? Yet the thought of behaving like a love-sick, wavering woman was nauseating to her. An empty sickness lay at the pit of her stomach. She drove home in a trance. Even the flat looked different in the light of this new experience, and the fact that, for the first time, she and Garth had become emotional strangers. The thought of getting a meal, or eating food of any kind, revolted her, and she sat staring at the Castle etched against the evening sky. The hours ahead seemed interminable. She switched on the television and went through all the channels with the remote control, finding nothing of any interest and turning it off in disgust. The ringing of the telephone made her jump, and she answered it a little breathlessly. Was it possible that Garth might ring?

But it was Elaine, saying apologetically, 'I'm so sorry, Andrea, to call you at home, but I wonder if you could have a look at me professionally tomorrow?'

Andrea felt immediate apprehension. She didn't want Elaine as a patient, yet she could hardly refuse, or, inevitably, Garth might be drawn into the picture.

'What seems to be wrong?' Andrea temporised.

'Abdominal pain.'

'You're not going to——'

'No! It isn't going to be an emergency appendix,' came the swift reply. 'Can I make an appointment when I get to surgery tomorrow?'

Andrea's thoughts were racing, but all she could say was, 'Do; I suggest lunch time. We could have a sandwich afterwards.' She added, 'Are you all right? Or would you like me to come round?'

'I'll survive until tomorrow,' came the light reply. 'Probably all tied up with an erratic menstrual cycle.' She went on pleasantly, 'Only doctors can give us reassurance, when it comes to it!'

Andrea replaced the receiver and was aware of the unease that always seemed to strike her whenever Elaine came into the picture. It didn't matter that they'd had months of smooth running in the practice, she always felt that suspense hung over Elaine's relationship with Garth, and it had never been stronger than at that moment.

After an almost sleepless night, Andrea met Garth in his consulting room the following morning as was customary, in order to discuss their daily routine and confer about problem cases.

'*Elaine!*' Garth said, almost alarmed when Andrea told him of the telephone call and the fact that she was seeing Elaine professionally at lunch time that day.

'So she hasn't mentioned it to you?'

'No,' he replied, inwardly wondering why, and a little surprised that she should want to be a patient in the practice. 'You know I prefer the staff to seek medical care elsewhere.'

Andrea could not help exclaiming, 'Elaine has not seemed to come into that category.'

She had not intended any innuendo, but he countered a trifle sharply, 'Nevertheless, she is an employee.'

'I don't really think we need give any significance to her coming to me.' She added, 'I assumed *you* would not wish to treat her.'

'Your assumption being correct.'

Andrea was painfully aware of him; the tension almost tangible as her longing increased and she wanted to rush to his arms and tell him how she felt. But that would surely be an embarrassment and a disaster. The most she could hope for was to keep peace between them and allow matters to take their course. Ironically, now that she was in love with him, she knew that she could not endure being made love to on the old terms. His withdrawn manner and general air of disapproval reinforced to belief that he, also, would have no wish to continue the intimacy.

Emotion, nevertheless, lay dangerously between them. They were alert and wary of each other.

Elaine spoke to Garth about her appointment with Andrea during the short break after surgery.

'Abdominal pain can be nothing,' she said dismissively, 'and I've put off doing anything about it.'

'Why didn't you go to see Dr Jayson, or his partner Mr Brian Newton?' Garth asked her. 'He's the gynae man.'

Elaine replied coolly, 'Because I prefer Andrea, and have great faith in her as a doctor. I didn't think it was a good idea to come to you.'

He ignored that by saying, 'I hope it is something simple . . . Take the rest of the day off, if you wish.'

She changed the mood, looking at him appealingly, her voice quiet and soft, 'I'd do that only if it were absolutely necessary . . . Have I been the help you hoped for when you decided to employ a nurse?'

Garth sensed danger. 'Yes, we've both been spared a great deal of work.' He rushed on, not wishing to prolong any personal exchanges, 'Now I've to go to Knighton Hospital to see old Mr Buxton who was taken there after a road accident this morning.'

'I'm sorry. I like Mr Buxton.' Again she attempted to draw Garth closer, and said wistfully, 'You pass the "Welcome to Wales" sign on the Knighton road.'

'I wonder you didn't remain in Wales,' he suggested without feeling.

Her gaze met his boldly. 'People mean more to me than places, Garth.' Seeing the frown that puckered his brow, she said hastily, 'You won't forget your appointment with Mr Winthrop at three.'

He sighed. He had forgotten. It was as though a vision of Andrea was permanently before his eyes, her attitude baffling and shattering.

'Thank you for reminding me,' he said more gently, adding, 'I hope all goes well with the appointment. Let me know how you get on.'

'I will,' she said, and there was a knowing little smile beneath her inscrutability. In some subtle and obscure fashion, she felt that she had made a little progress. The last thing she wanted was to be ill, but requiring a little attention would not be amiss . . .

Andrea accepted Elaine as a patient, intent only on making the right diagnosis. She had considerable respect for Elaine's knowledge as a nurse, and knew that she would not accept anything other than the truth.

Elaine said factually and without preamble, 'I've fluctuating pain and a swelling in the lower abdomen. In fact, when I look at myself in the bathroom mirror, I might almost be pregnant!' She laughed. 'I can assure you that I'm not.'

'Any intermittent menstrual bleeding?' Andrea asked.

'No; but I've never been very regular . . . Oh!' She paused. 'I had a miscarriage at fourteen weeks during the year Ralph and I were married. I wouldn't call myself an over-maternal person, but we were both very sorry. Apart from that, I've been disgustingly healthy and never needed a doctor.'

'Let's have a look at you.'

Elaine undressed and got on the examining couch.

'Everything seems very different from here,' she said with a wry smile. 'I'm usually at your end!'

Andrea's hands moved slowly and surely over her abdomen, having taken her temperature, pulse, blood pressure; finally making a pelvic examination, and said eventually, 'Get dressed, and we'll talk.'

'I think this may well be an ovarian cyst,' Andrea said as they faced each other again over her desk. 'You've probably suspected it.' She looked at the nurse levelly.

Elaine nodded. 'I'd listed it among the possibilities;

but, when it comes to it, my knowledge is limited.'

'I'd like you to have a Real Time scan. That way we shall be completely in the picture and can take it from there.'

'And they can tell if the cyst is benign,' Elaine announced without dramatics.

'Almost certainly.'

'I know the procedure for that scan. A full bladder, and they put gel all over your abdomen, then an acoustic coupler removes air between the ultrasound transducer and the skin!' Elain laughed. 'I've know patients to come with an empty bladder and have had to sit and drink masses of fluid before they could be done. I intended specialising in radiology. I'm sorry . . . you don't want extraneous details!'

'But it's a welcome change to deal with a patient who can speak one's own language.'

'It will mean an operation?'

'More than likely.'

Elaine shook her head. 'I could do without all the fuss.' She looked at Andrea gratefully. 'I'm so relieved to have you for my doctor. Makes it all so much simpler . . . Who would do the operation?'

'Dr Jayson's partner, Mr Brian Newton. Dr Jayson specialises in radiology, and you can see him at the hospital.'

Elaine introduced a personal note. 'You and Dr Jayson are good friends.'

It was a question asked as a statement.

'Very,' Andrea said, clinging to the comfort of Douglas's love for her and feeling the warmth of his friendship.

'I've only spoken to him on the telephone. He has an attractive voice.'

All Andrea could hear at that moment was the echo of Garth's cold forbidding tone, and her heart felt heavy, her stomach empty, her mouth dry. She resented his power over her, and saw that Elaine was watching her with speculation.

'I don't know of many practices similar to yours and Garth's. Not with just one man and one woman in it. Garth is an unusual man, isn't he?'

Andrea did not want to discuss Garth, and yet was almost hypnotised into doing so. There was a significance in Elaine's tone that arrested her attention.

'We are all a mass of contradictions,' Andrea replied evasively.

'Each with a story to tell,' Elaine added. 'Now that you're my doctor, it's amazing how different I feel. I've acquired a confidante who will keep all my secrets!'

'"Secrets"?' Andrea echoed, forcing an unnatural laugh as tension mounted. 'I am concerned only with your medical history, Elaine.'

Elaine studied Andrea very carefully, just as she had studied her, quietly and unobtrusively, since becoming the nurse at Clee View. The blinking of Andrea's eyes, the slight flush that mounted her cheeks at the mention of Garth's name . . . She was in love with him, Elaine decided, sensing danger; a danger she had always foreseen, yet curiously enough had refused to accept as an open challenge, her conceit too great, since she prided herself that only her own deviousness and scheming enabled the practice to run harmoniously.

'I thought doctors insisted on treating the whole person? All you know about me is that I am a widow.'

Andrea said swiftly, 'It is enough to deal with simple facts unless, of course, there are any disturbing factors likely to have a psychological effect on the patient.'

It was the opening Elaine sought.

'I need someone to confide in: someone I can trust absolutely. One's doctor is one's priest, after all.' She paused dramatically, then, 'You see, Garth and I are not strangers. We knew each other a few years ago. He insisted that no one should be told.'

An electric silence fell. All the fears Andrea had experienced, suspicious, nebulous, fleeting, and without direction, tumbled out like objects from a magician's box. Elaine's words echoed like the wind whining through a forest on a dark stormy night, bringing a sick disillusionment.

'I see,' Andrea said in a breath.

'You looked shocked. I thought you would have guessed . . . We were lovers who ought never to have parted. If you only knew what a relief it is to be able to tell you! It isn't like betraying any secrets to talk to you.'

Andrea felt trapped. Every nerve in her body seemed to be painful, her heart thumping, her thoughts chaotic. It was like watching a world, a relationship, disintegrate. Yet now everything fell into place, making her marvel at her own naïvety and gullibility: Garth's erratic attitude, his behaviour when he and Elaine met again.

'I don't see how this has any bearing on your present condition,' Andrea managed to say calmly. 'It is none of my business.' Her voice hardened slightly, 'And, since Garth didn't want it discussed . . .'

'Ah, but you're different.'

'He didn't think so, or he would have told me.' The words tumbled out on a note of pain, and Andrea struggled to retrieve them by hastening, 'We haven't made it our business to discuss our respective pasts. They've no bearing whatever on the present.'

Elaine's voice had a purring note, 'Not to *you*, but to

me, since that past, in Garth's and my case, is by no means dead. Emotional involvement——'

Those two words pierced Andrea's heart like a dagger, since she had so foolishly used them herself, the bitterness of regret shrivelling her even as she sat there.

Elaine held Andrea's gaze deliberately, 'I'm sorry, Andrea. I feel I've upset you in some way by confiding all this.'

Andrea's spine stiffened, and control and courage returned as she said with a faint laugh, 'My dear Elaine, I'm far more interested in your possible cyst than in your past. I'm Garth's partner, not his keeper. You surely don't think that I imagined he'd never had any affairs!' She smiled, and rushed on before Elaine had time to speak, 'Men just don't discuss them, that's all.'

Elaine's temper was flaming beneath the surface, and she spoke through clenched teeth, 'I was not suggesting for a moment that Garth and I had an affair.'

Andrea looked suitably apologetic, and replied, 'I'm sorry; forgive me . . . Now to come back to the important thing. I'll have a word with Dr Jayson, and get his partner to have a look at you and arrange the scan.'

Elaine's emotions were chaotic. She couldn't tell quite how, or why, but it seemed that Andrea had scored a victory when she, herself, had set out to triumph. She said, almost on a note of command, 'And I'd rather you didn't discuss my case with Garth. *I* shall do that.'

Andrea merely nodded.

Elaine calmed down. She might not have triumphed now, but she would do so in the future, she told herself with certitude. Andrea was not an easy opponent, and if she was in love with Garth, she certainly handled the fact with aplomb. Elaine turned on the charm as she got up from the patients' chair.

'You've been so helpful, Andrea, and I'm more than grateful. I feel wretched about all this. It will mean my being away from here if I need an op . . . How long?'

'A month's sick leave,' Andrea said, her voice smooth and understanding. 'The operation itself will take only twenty to thirty minutes, as you well know.'

'I forget . . . How long should I be in hospital?'

'About six days.'

'I shall hate not being able to work!'

Andrea laughed. 'One doesn't very often hear that said!'

'Circumstances alter cases,' Elaine murmured. 'Thank you again. You've been very kind.'

And all Andrea could think of as the door shut behind her was that Elaine and Garth had been lovers. Why hadn't he told her? Why had he allowed her to remain in ignorance? It seemed a treachery, cheapening their relationship. And why didn't he want Elaine to tell the truth? Was it because he feared to endanger his convenient relationship with her, Andrea? Thus he preserved the best of both worlds. Nothing added up, and she sat there staring into space.

When Garth had been to Knighton Hospital and then seen Mr Winthrop at three, he looked in on Andrea, who was studying The *Practitioner* in a ten-minute lull in the afternoon appointment list. Trying to bring back a little normality, he asked, 'How did you get on with Elaine?' His voice was quietly professional. He didn't sit down.

'She doesn't wish me to discuss her case with you,' Andrea said evenly, her gaze steady.

'Good lord, why?' The words came naturally.

'You should know the answer,' Andrea retorted,

emotion choking her. 'She prefers to tell you the details herself.'

'But . . .' He was going to protest, and then stopped, circumstances dictating his reticence as he continued a little awkwardly, 'Oh, very well.'

Andrea's expression was stony, her eyes meeting his as desire battled against jealousy, anger, and even scorn. He could have told her the truth about Elaine. Whatever excuses she might want to make for him, that fact stood out glaringly, cutting across any possibility of forgiveness. Of course she had not expected him to live a celibate life in the past, but she did expect a degree of frankness had there been anything serious and which intruded into the present. Elaine's return made it a point of honour, she considered, and his wishing to keep the past a secret, belittled him. Yet why didn't despising him take away the heartache, anguish and longing? It would be so easy to convince herself that the attraction between them was as great as ever, and that were she to give him one word of encouragement, his arms would be around her . . . All the time Elaine was, and had been, in the background, their relationship suspect. *'We were lovers who ought never to have parted.'* Her body shivered in a wave of distaste as she thought of Elaine in his arms . . . Had he been making love to her while *they* were together? She remembered the promise they had made to each other that there would not be anyone else while their relationship lasted. Would he have argued that Elaine was different—like a wife, to whom he was being unfaithful?

He said sharply, 'Are you all right, Andrea? You look so strained—upset . . . Surely our misunderstanding . . .' He floundered, abashed by her flint-like gaze. He burst out fiercely, his voice hoarse and accusing, 'If

Douglas is at the bottom of your sudden change of attitude, surely to goodness you can be honest with me!'

'And honesty means so much to you!' The words seemed to tumble out of their own accord, and she covered them up by adding swiftly, 'To us both. If I decide to marry Douglas, you will be the first to know. I think I've already told you that.' She hated being at a disadvantage, Elaine's confidence hanging over her menacingly. The wrong word, and that confidence would be betrayed, her professional honour forfeited.

The intercom went. Andrea's patient was waiting.

Elaine appeared at the open doorway at that moment.

'Could you spare me five minutes, Garth?' She smiled at Andrea, and Andrea felt cold as she reflected that she and Elaine shared a secret that placed Garth at a disadvantage, making frankness with him doubly impossible. Where, before, she could have dealt with her love for him and ended their relationship with dignity, now she found herself despising not only him, but herself, for the manner in which she had handled the situation.

Garth's face held a dark, almost threatening anger, as he turned away from Andrea, and said, 'By all means.' They left the room together.

Elaine explained the facts to Garth, who expressed his regret that there was the possibility of an operation being necessary, adding, despite himself, 'Andrea is a very good diagnostician.'

'I shall loathe being away from here and having all the palaver that always goes with ops, no matter for what they may be.'

'We shall miss you,' Garth said straightforwardly, thinking purely of the work and hoping that Elaine's case would not present any complications.

Elaine's expression was tender and all-embracing as she said, 'Will you replace me?'

He started, 'Meaning . . . ?' He stopped, sensing that Elaine was seeking reassurance.

'I mean, while I'm away.'

'No,' he said firmly. 'By the time anyone else had grown accustomed to the job, you would be back, and I don't like newcomers around the place.'

Elaine had been granted just the opportunity she wanted. 'What will you do when Andrea leaves you?' She watched with bitter jealousy the alarm that flashed into Garth's eyes.

'"Leaves"?' His voice was shaken. 'What do you mean?'

'Well, when she and Douglas marry.' It was a shot in the dark, for Elaine had no justification whatever for the suggestion.

Garth stiffened. 'I wasn't aware that they were going to *be* married,' he said, shocked.

'There's none so blind . . . !' Elaine said with a slow significant smile.

The thought of losing Andrea (even though he had discussed the subject of Douglas with her only a matter of minutes ago) sent a wave of acute distress and depression over him. He was at a loss to understand Andrea's attitude, and fearful lest there might be some truth in Elaine's remarks.

He snapped, 'Don't be ridiculous, Elaine.'

'Nevertheless, you do wear blinkers,' she said teasingly. 'Andrea was the perfect doctor to me today, but she's very much on edge and erratic—a typical "woman in love" sign. Perhaps she's only just realised how she feels about him.'

Garth shuddered. Wouldn't that explain Andrea's

changed mood; her reluctance to go out with *him*—her whole attitude? Was it that she wanted to finish her relationship with himself, and didn't quite know how to go about it? Elaine was a shrewd and discerning person and very little escaped her notice, he reflected gloomily.

'I do not wish to discuss Andrea.' He spoke sharply. 'You will see Dr Jayson and Mr Newton, and be advised by them as to the next step. I'm sorry about it all. But a cyst can be a very simple thing.'

'With many permutations.' She looked a little forlorn. 'Will you visit me when I'm in hospital? I've no one, Garth.' She paused, and then added swiftly, 'And would you come and have a drink with me this evening? You did promise to come to see the house after it was furnished, but you never have. Surely, now, we can relax and understand each other?'

Garth's attitude softened slightly; he had, he knew, been almost unnecessarily harsh, but now the thought of Andrea and Douglas whipped up what he knew to be an unreasoning fury. He replied almost belligerently, 'Very well. I know I promised to have a look at the house again, particularly as I was instrumental in your buying the smaller one.'

'I deliberately haven't tried to persuade you,' she reminded him quietly.

He appreciated that she had been the soul of discretion during these months, and felt a little mean.

'You have lived up to your bargain.' His voice was gentler.

Elaine thrilled to his change of attitude, her love for him deepening, her determination to become a part of his life the ultimate goal in her carefully devised plan. These months had been refined torture, as she had watched the obvious attraction between him and

Andrea, always waiting for the right opportunity to strike, if not a fatal blow, then one which would have serious repercussions. She intended to be Mrs Garth Howard, and it would take more than Andrea to stop her. Andrea was, she reflected, a fine character, but she was also the type to retreat in the face of opposition, not capable of stooping to any underhanded tactics, or combat carefully planned deceits. And Elaine had no illusions: Andrea was in love with Garth. She refused to contemplate the possibility that he might reciprocate her feelings. Were that so, they would be either engaged, or married. Her thoughts flew on . . . Nothing could serve her own purpose better than to have Andrea as her doctor, her *confidante*.

Garth saw Andrea again as they were leaving their respective rooms after surgery.

'One moment,' he said, speaking from his doorway as she reached it from the corridor.

Andrea moved forward as he stepped back to allow her to enter. He remained standing.

'Would it inconvenience you to have the calls transferred to your home number for a couple of hours this evening?'

Their eyes met and there were memories in the gaze. For her, memories of lying in his arms, feeling his strong body against hers, his kiss exciting and thrilling. *Would it inconvenience you?* Was it possible that it was Garth speaking? That they were standing there, awkwardly, a world apart, as he moved a few paces away?

'Not at all,' she replied, and now her voice was quiet and calm. The storm had died down in the wake of acceptance. She loved him, but now knew him for what he was. She could either walk out of the practice, or remain and behave in a purely professional manner.

And she knew that she hadn't the courage, at this stage, to face up to a final parting, no matter how incongruous the circumstances.

'Thank you.'

She wondered if he would tell her the reason for the request, but he said no more and averted his eyes as he walked towards his desk. The silence was heavy and unnerving.

'What time will you ask to go on transfer?'

'Could I make it about seven-thirty . . . ?' He corrected himself. 'No, say seven-fifteen?'

'Very well.'

Andrea was shaking as she left him, feeling ill and sick at heart, as though she had suffered a bereavement. Elaine caught up with her as she reached the front door.

'By the way,' Elaine said brightly, 'did Garth remember to ask you to hold the fort this evening?'

Andrea tensed and nodded.

'Only he can be so absent-minded, and he's coming to me for drinks. I didn't feel well enough to go out tonight.'

NO STAMP NEEDED

To Susan Welland
Mills & Boon
Reader Service
FREEPOST
P.O. Box 236
CROYDON
Surrey CR9 9EL.

FREE BOOKS CERTIFICATE

Dear Susan,

Your special Introductory offer of 12 Free books is too good to miss. I understand they are mine to keep with the free necklace.

Please also reserve a Reader Service Subscription for me. If I decide to subscribe, I shall, from the beginning of the month following my free parcel of books, receive 12 new books each month for £14.40, post and packing free. If I decide not to subscribe, I shall write to you within 10 days. The free books will be mine to keep.

I understand that I may cancel my subscription at any time simply by writing to you. I am over 18 years of age.

10A6TA

Name _____ Signature _____
(BLOCK CAPITALS PLEASE)
Address _____

Postcode _____

Offer applies in the UK and Eire, overseas send for details. Mills & Boon Ltd. reserve the right to exercise discretion in granting membership. Should a price change become necessary you will be notified. You may be mailed with other offers as a result of this application. Offer expires 31st March 1987.

Open your heart to Love
with 12 Romances Free
your welcome gift from Mills & Boon

Love, romance, intrigue...all are captured for you by Mills & Boon's top selling authors. By becoming a regular reader of Mills & Boon's romances you can enjoy twelve superb new titles every month plus a whole range of special benefits: your very own personal membership card, a free monthly newsletter packed with recipes, competitions, exclusive book offers and a monthly guide to the stars, plus extra bargain offers and big cash savings.

As a special introduction we will send you 12 exciting Mills & Boon Romances and a diamond zirconia necklace FREE when you complete and return this card.

At the same time we will reserve a subscription to Mills & Boon Reader Service for you. Every month, you will receive twelve of the very latest novels by leading Romantic Fiction authors, delivered direct to your door. And they cost just the same as they would in the shops – postage and packing is always completely Free. There is no obligation or commitment – you can cancel your subscription at any time.

It's so easy! Send no money now – you don't even need a stamp. Just fill in and detach this card and send it off today.

plus an attractive
DIAMOND ZIRCONIA NECKLACE FREE

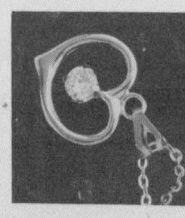

CHAPTER SIX

ANDREA felt that many years, rather than hours, had passed between seeing Elaine as a patient and returning to her flat that evening. Had she been blind during those summer months, believing that Garth's business-like attitude towards Elaine was perfectly genuine, instead of a façade to conceal a deeper relationship? A relationship renewed from the past and increasing in intensity? She could not dismiss his visit to Elaine that evening as a kindly gesture stimulated by concern for her physical condition.

When the doorbell rang, she answered it, almost hoping that it might be an emergency to break into her turbulent thoughts, but it was Douglas, saying, 'I've just come from a midder . . . Any hope of wetting the baby's head?'

'For the second time?' she laughed, genuinely pleased to see him.

'No, the parents were teetotallers! Quite a new experience.' He stared at her critically. 'It won't please you, if I say you look tired.'

'It's a tactful way of telling me that I've aged since you last saw me!'

They went into the sitting room and she indicated the drinks tray. 'I'll join you in the brandy . . . Boy or girl?'

He chuckled. 'I didn't realise brandy had a sex! Girl. They have two boys.'

Andrea thought, how fantastic life is! Here I am, smiling, hopeful of making sense, when all the time I feel

I'm dying a little inside, and all I can really think of is Garth with Elaine. What will they be saying? Doing? The secrecy on his part was an indictment she could not bear.

'I'm on call.' She glanced at the telephone. 'On transfer.'

'I haven't seen Garth for nearly three weeks,' Douglas said, puzzled. 'He's been damned elusive this summer . . . Where is he tonight?' It was a question asked bluntly by a friend not apologising for the curiosity.

'Elaine said he was having a drink with her.'

Douglas looked surprised. 'I'm sorry that she needs to consult me,' he said, changing the subject. 'But I'm glad we could fit the appointment in tomorrow. Sorry, also, I wasn't able to speak to you when you telephoned.'

'Good heavens,' Andrea exclaimed, 'I didn't hope to get you. Hospital day, isn't it?'

'So you do think of me enough to remember my consultant rota! I'm flattered. You've seemed miles away these past weeks.' He had poured out the brandies and settled himself in an armchair opposite her. 'But because I've not chased you, it doesn't mean my intentions have changed. Let's make a day of it, sometime. Go into Shrewsbury—anywhere.'

Andrea said defiantly, 'I'd like that.' But she meant it. Douglas lifted her spirits and made her feel that she was standing on solid ground. He was a man to marry; to entrust one's life to without fear, his loyalty absolute.

'If you'd say "Yes", we could make it an engagement celebration,' he suggested, smiling.

Impulsively, heart racing, she said, 'I'll give you my answer then.'

'And when will "then" be?'

'As soon as we can both manage a day off—We must synchronise our times.'

'Ah! I see your point,' he exclaimed ruefully.

Andrea found herself saying, without quite knowing why, 'There has been someone in my life, Douglas. I don't want to pretend, or deceive you in any way. Not an emotional involvement.' She tried not to make the words sound ironical.

He didn't look either shocked, or surprised.

'I'm asking for the present and future, not for promises about the past. All the same, I appreciate you telling me. I hardly think you'd believe me if I said I'd lived a celibate life.'

She gave a little laugh. Why, she asked herself, couldn't she have accepted Garth's relationship with Elaine with the same nonchalance? Because, her thoughts raced, she loved him, and there was the searing fear that the association was not confined to yesterday.

The telephone rang and she picked it up, alerted as she said, 'Mr Ranleigh?'

'Please come, Doctor! I think my wife's having a heart attack.'

'I'll be with you.' The Ranleigh house was on the Richard's Castle road, only a short distance away.

Douglas got to his feet and picked up her medical bag which was lying on the sofa, handing it to her, and saying helpfully, 'I'll stay here until you get back. You can ring me if there's a serious problem. Brian's taking care of things my end, and knows where I am.' He added protectively, 'It's cold out.'

She grabbed a coat from the bedroom and was gone.

Mr Ranleigh, white-faced, a man of nearing sixty, answered Andrea's ring as her finger touched the bell.

'Thank God you're here!' He talked as they made

their way up a reasonably wide staircase. 'She's been having indigestion lately, but you know what she is, will never give in——'

Mrs Ranleigh, a chocolate-box-pretty fair-haired woman of fifty, was propped up on several pillows, one hand pressing just below the sternum and the other holding her throat. Her speech was shaky and slow, 'I was coming to see you . . . Indigestion . . .'

Andrea was accustomed to 'indigestion' and the trap it set for all doctors. She made a thorough examination, satisfying herself that this was not a case for hospital but for investigation, since so many symptoms simulated complaints that had very little to do with the ultimate diagnosis. She was only too conscious that a hiatus hernia could appear as angina, or duodenal trouble.

'How long have you had the indigestion?' Andrea put away her sphygmomanometer and stethoscope. 'And heartburn,' she added.

'Oh, quite a time; it wasn't bad at first.' She breathed more deeply. 'It's easier now . . .'

'Take your time, Mrs Ranleigh.'

'I'd got to like spicy foods. My daughter—you know Polly!—Well, she and her husband came home on leave from Hong Kong in the spring . . . They cooked a lot of spicy things which didn't agree with me, and I put it down to that.' She looked at Andrea half-apologetically, and said disjointedly, 'Recently, it's been different; the pain just here'—she touched her oesophagus—'the burning when I stoop; and my heart, well it's been frightening. Seems to move about in my chest. I can feel it; and the beats are so irregular . . . Then it rights itself.'

Andrea nodded; she had her fingers on Mrs Ranleigh's pulse.

'I got some Gaviscon tablets . . .'

'They would help indigestion,' Andrea agreed, not ruling out the possibility of a hiatus hernia—a protrusion of part of the stomach through the diaphragm at the weakest part where the oesophagus passes. 'I want a thorough investigation, Mrs Ranleigh. An ECG, to begin with, and a possible oesophagoscopy. This is an examination by an instrument like a small telescope passed down your oesophagus.'

'It isn't a coronary?' There was anxiety in the blue eyes.

'No . . . Now I want you to rest.'

'I can't lie down . . . Everything seems to rise into my throat, and water comes into my mouth.' Her voice was less jerky and a little stronger, her sigh apologetic. 'I haven't spared anyone anything by putting off coming to you,' she said regretfully.

'Patients seldom do,' Andrea said, gently but ruefully.

'It's just that one knows how *busy* you are . . . But this is—is different.' She added, 'I scared my poor husband!'

'You don't want *him* to have the coronary,' Andrea suggested with a half-smile, 'so from now on you must do as you're told. I'll ring you first thing in the morning, and we'll get the ECG done.'

Mr Ranleigh came back into the room. Andrea's presence had removed the fears of a crisis.

Andrea asked unexpectedly, and despite the fact that Mrs Ranleigh had cut out spicy foods, 'What did you have to eat this evening?'

'A made-up dish with onions,' Mr Ranleigh said.

Andrea patted Mrs Ranleigh's arm. 'The wrong thing, but it merely aggravated a condition we must deal with.' She smiled indulgently, thankful and relieved that there had been an improvement in Mrs Ranleigh's cardiac tone during the short time she had been there.

A short while later she returned to the flat, where Douglas was watching the weather forecast at the end of the nine o'clock news.

'Well?' he said, switching it off as he got up out of his chair.

She explained.

'Always tricky,' he said with understanding. 'And you can't give any cast-iron opinion until you've had the tests done. Oh, by the way, and before I forget, Garth telephoned.'

'Why?' she asked stupidly, her heart racing. That Douglas was there would be significant from Garth's point of view. She hastened, 'I mean . . .'

'To tell you he was back on call, and make sure there had been no emergencies. We were able to catch up on the news, and we're going to get together at the first opportunity,' he added easily.

'Oh, good,' Andrea said, depression seeping into her like fog on a winter's night. It didn't seem possible that she and Garth had reached a stage in their relationship where neither knew the other's plans, except by vicarious means. Douglas's presence would merely confirm his previous suspicions, because of what she recognised as her intransigent behaviour. Nothing could alter the fact that she had handled the situation foolishly, and had no means of redeeming it except by confessing her love for Garth. The hurt, unhappiness and depression were twice as great because she had only herself to blame for the present chaos, no matter what his relationship with Elaine might be at the moment.

Garth said the following morning, coming into her room before surgery, 'I'm sorry your evening was disrupted. Nothing very serious, I hope?'

She explained, and sought his approval for arranging the tests.

'One can never take anything for granted,' he said supportively. 'You're quite right. When in doubt, don't ignore any symptoms.' His gaze held hers. 'At least I was able to have a chat with Douglas.'

Andrea willed him to mention Elaine, to confide his plans, introduce some personal note. But all he said was, 'Elaine will be with him now.'

'Yes,' she said, jealousy like a spike in her heart. His remark showed where his thoughts were.

Silence, full of suspense and tension, fell.

'Andrea?' He uttered her name in a sudden whisper, emotion surging between them as their eyes met with questioning appeal.

The intercom went.

'Damn!'

Andrea was trembling as she heard him say, 'Yes, very well. Let surgery begin.' She hurried to the door without looking back, and before he had time to say anything more. The appeal of his low, almost intimate, voice shattered her control and she dared not trust herself to speak.

Douglas greeted Elaine with a studied, questioning look as he shook hands and then indicated the patients' chair, his gaze never leaving her face; not with the assessment of a doctor, but of someone trying to search their memory for recollection.

'We've met somewhere before, Nurse Drake,' he said as they sat down. 'I flatter myself that I never forget a face, but for the life of me I cannot remember where.'

Elaine said honestly, but with the breath of fear, 'I'm sure I've never met *you* before, Dr Jayson, and I also flatter myself. You may have some cinema or television personality in mind. It happens all the time, these days!'

'Not to me it doesn't,' he said with a light laugh. 'I have little time for either . . . I shall remember when I least expect it . . . Now it's a question of confirming Dr Forbes's diagnosis.'

Elaine said deliberately, 'I have enormous respect for Dr Forbes's judgment.' And, even as she spoke, she was searching her memory to discover just where this man might have met her, and what dangers might be entailed. An ovarian cyst seemed of little importance by comparison.

After he had examined her, he said, 'Dr Forbes's diagnosis is correct, and in my opinion we should operate.' He looked at her with frank assessment, 'I don't have to tell you, as a nurse, the possibilities.'

'No,' she agreed. 'I've seen too much first hand, and I prefer to know. The "nasties" grow rapidly and spread to other organs, and we don't want the ovaries themselves involved.'

'Fortunately,' Douglas said, aware that it was easy to be over-dramatic, 'this—what I believe to be your condition—is very common and dealt with very simply. I'd like you to have a Real Time scan and get the whole picture. Mr Newton will arrange that at the hospital.'

'Thank you. But, after that, I'd like to have the operation done at Merrifields Nursing Home, which I know you attend.'

'Of course that can be arranged,' he said, 'but . . .'

'I've had enough of hospitals,' she interrupted firmly, 'I want it over and done with.'

Douglas appreciated that, more than her manner. There was just something about Nurse Drake that didn't appeal to him. He could imagine her being an excellent nurse, highly intelligent, who was too tactful to air her knowledge in a supercilious manner, while making it known that she was fully aware of all the ramifications of her particular condition. He gave her the benefit of the doubt when it came to their having met, because her gaze had been blank and in no way simulated ignorance. He didn't quite know why it appeared so important to remember where he had previously seen her.

Douglas made the appointment with Brian Newton, and she said, 'I can rely on you yourself performing the operation, Dr Jayson?'

'Certainly, if that is your wish. I'll arrange with the nursing home and get you in as quickly as possible.'

'I don't want to be away from the practice for longer than is strictly necessary,' she said emphatically. 'As you know only too well, we're coming up to the busiest time, although with the population movement we're dealing with more and more viruses and bugs with which we are unfamiliar.' She smiled. 'Some holiday patients pay dearly for their dose of sun.'

'I'm sure Dr Howard would agree to your having a holiday in it, nevertheless,' Douglas suggested.

Her smile was slow and secretive. 'He knows I wouldn't extend my sick leave a minute longer than necessary!' She got to her feet, her slow smile, her bold dark eyes, direct and challenging.

Where, Douglas asked himself again, had he met her, and when? As she left, he reflected that Nurse Drake was the type who, when she wanted a thing, would break all the rules to get it. And he hoped Garth would not become involved with her . . .

Elaine reported back to Andrea, and when she had explained the arrangements, asked, 'Is Garth free?'

'I don't know,' Andrea replied.

'It doesn't matter, in any case. He's going to look in to see me at lunch time and didn't want me to work today. The discomfort isn't too pleasant!' She said with a rather woebegone expression, 'Would you tell him I've gone home? I'll be thankful when the op's done . . . He's a pleasant sort of man, Dr Jayson.' She met Andrea's gaze. 'But definitely not like Garth . . . No sex appeal!'

Garth came into Andrea's room at that moment, addressing Elaine, 'Mrs Boyer told me you were back.'

Elaine repeated what had been said, adding, 'I'll tell you all about it later on. I'm going home now. I feel lousy, to be honest, and will take your advice.' She was not making a fuss for effect, and both he and Andrea realised it. 'I'll take a couple of Distalgesic.'

'Would you like one of us to drive you home?'

She shook her head. 'I'd have to be dying not to be able to drive,' she exclaimed, and moved towards the door. Andrea noticed the way Garth put a hand on her elbow, his solicitude obvious, the words, '*He's going to look in to see me at lunch time*', stinging.

Garth returned to the room. 'I shall be glad when she's had the scan . . . Looks pretty washed out.'

'Yes, I'm sorry. Thank goodness she's healthy in every other way.'

Their eyes met with professional understanding; there was often a terrible irony in those words. In those seconds, they were two doctors discussing a case.

Garth recalled Elaine's gentle sympathetic manner the previous evening, more than ever feeling guilty because he had misjudged her motives in returning to his life. She had not intruded, and he felt it only humanitarian to show her kindness and consideration now, giving her the friendship she genuinely sought as she endeavoured to rebuild her life. He was at a disadvantage with Andrea after his definite stand about no social fraternising, and her somewhat cynical and accusing attitude had not stimulated any desire to be frank. After all, why should he have explained about his visit to Elaine? Andrea had not mentioned that she was seeing Douglas. And even though the whole issue seemed petty, he knew that such pettiness was the threat to all relationships, no matter what their nature. It was easy enough to see a failing, but not so easy to rectify it. Pride and a degree of stubbornness embittered him. His emotional life seemed to lie in ruins as though some invisible hand had destroyed it. He could not have defined his feelings or his motives as he exclaimed, 'Elaine is a very lonely person.'

'One cannot make friends *for* her,' Andrea retorted. 'She has your friendship these days, and I'm sure she finds that very satisfying.' She got up from her desk as she spoke, emotion tearing at her and mingling with annoyance. Was he suggesting tacitly that she should pander to Elaine, and build up the operation into some drama? 'Now, if you'll excuse me, I've a report to dictate.' She switched on the intercom to summon Mrs Boyer.

Garth stared at her, turned on his heel, and left.

She sat there in an alternating state of dumb misery and blazing fury. '*Elaine is a very lonely person.*' Wasn't it becoming obvious that he was still attracted to her, if not in love with her? She was staggered by his volte-face.

It was at lunch time that he said, as Andrea was about to have a coffee and sandwich in her room, 'I'm looking in on Elaine.' There was a note of defiance in his voice and a faintly warning expression on his face.

'She said you were.' Andrea stared him out coldly,

tacitly implying that she was well aware of his movements. 'Douglas has already fixed for her to go to Merrifields at the weekend, so that ordeal will soon be over.' She sipped her coffee. 'He'll operate on Monday. I've just had a word with him. She has an appointment with Brian at twelve o'clock tomorrow. He had a cancellation, fortunately.'

'Oh, good.'

Andrea made no further effort at conversation, and he hovered for a second before leaving. To her amazement, he reappeared and stood holding the door ajar.

'I'm coming to see you this evening,' he said with authority. 'I won't keep you long. About seven.'

He had gone before she had time to protest.

Garth gave Elaine Andrea's message about the nursing home, and she heaved a sigh of relief. 'Patience is not one of my few virtues,' she admitted. 'When it comes to myself, I hate anything wrong, no matter how trivial it may be. And in our profession we live with the possibilities, not merely the symptoms . . . Andrea has been splendid.' She watched his expression carefully. 'And I can't tell you what your kindness has meant. By the way, how long have you known Dr Jayson?'

'Douglas? Since I came here. Why?'

'I wondered if you might have met him before then, or been associated in any way. In London, for instance, in your student days.'

'Good lord, no. We struck up an easy kind of friendship when I came here, and help each other out on occasion. But we don't socialise a great deal when it comes to it. We have the odd meal together, but there are no hard and fast rules.'

'And I suppose Andrea got to know him through the practice?'

Garth hesitated. Come to think of it, he himself had not stimulated Douglas's and Andrea's friendship; it had grown out of their professional association. 'I suppose you could say that.'

'So she didn't know him either, before she came to Ludlow?'

Garth laughed, and then his brows puckered. 'Why the interest?'

'Just woman's curiosity,' she said, feeling relieved by his answers. 'He and Andrea seem very suited . . . Oh, Garth, I've made some sandwiches,' she hurried on, not wanting him to think that she was introducing Douglas's and Andrea's names with any ulterior motive, 'and the coffee's ready. I know you'll forgive my not having prepared anything more substantial.'

'You shouldn't have troubled. Rest is . . .'

'. . . such a bore,' she said wearily. 'I hate not being at work.'

He looked at his watch. 'I have very little time, Elaine.'

'A sandwich won't take a minute, and they're here, ready.' She lifted a cover from a dish to expose beautifully arranged egg sandwiches.

'Your favourite,' she said. 'Not quite hard-boiled and just with salt!' She brought in the coffee percolator without dwelling on the previous remark, sat down rather breathlessly and allowed him to pour out and hand her a plate and napkin. But she knew that her recollection had stirred him, the anger dispersing with time.

As he was about to leave her a little later, she leaned forward and implanted a kiss lightly on his cheek. 'Thank you for coming . . . It will make the rest of the day bearable.'

He drove away, bewildered and apprehensive. This was the beguiling Elaine of the past, and sadness descended upon him as memories flooded back.

That evening Andrea showered and changed into an amber cashmere dress, brushed out her hair so that it cascaded almost shoulder length, and turned up the central heating to allow for the chill of a September evening that had nothing to recommend it. She was restless and uneasy. Suppose Garth wanted to dissolve their partnership? The possibility darted through her mind like a flashing spear. Suppose, on the other hand, he was coming to tell her the truth about Elaine and their relationship? Her heart-beats quickened, and hope sent a shiver of happiness over her as the doorbell rang. It had been a long while since he had visited her, and he came in as a stranger. He looked handsome as he stood in the glow of the wall lamps, noticing how beautiful she was, how dark and lustrous her eyes were. He liked the way she wore her clothes, with a casual elegance that removed any artificiality.

They settled in their respective chairs; chairs in which they had sat both before, and after, making love in those halcyon days that seemed to have been part of another life. In her confusion she forgot to mention the drinks, and then indicated the tray with an almost nervous, 'Will you?'

He got to his feet immediately, indicated a decanter and said, 'Sherry?'

'Please.'

He poured himself a whisky and set the glasses down on the respective occasional tables. Andrea dreaded having to pick her glass up because her hands were trembling. The atmosphere seemed alive with an emotion that was stormy and on the edge of hostility. Their eyes met, dark, half-accusing—two people poised on a precipice of indecision, passion and, above all, desire held in check until reaching a point of pain.

He said without preamble, 'I must know if you want to dissolve our partnership, Andrea.'

And although she had considered the possibility of *his* wishing to do so, the shock of his question shattered her.

'Dissolve it?' she repeated, feeling that he must hear her heart thudding.

'You sound surprised!' His voice dropped.

'Is this your way of getting rid of me?' The words were out before she realised their implications, or how they could be linked to their past relationship.

'Don't answer my question by asking another,' he said curtly.

A lump came into Andrea's throat. She had never loved him so deeply as in that moment when he seemed absolutely lost to her; when the distance between them both physically and mentally appeared as wide as an ocean. She wanted to cry out, 'I love you—Are you so blind that you can't see that?' Why should he even think of their parting unless his own desires stimulated the suggestion? She managed to gulp a little sherry, playing for time, feeling that, if she tried to speak, her voice would be so shaken as to be unintelligible and then, breathing deeply, said, 'Then my answer is no.' She knew, even as she spoke, that she was making the wrong decision. As things were, far better to retreat gracefully and lose the war than to keep on in silent battle with her love forever a stumbling block. Were Elaine not in the picture, it would have been so easy to fight in the hope of winning his love. With her, and the past as reinforcement for any plan she might have in mind, it was doomed.

Silence fell: a silence in which they looked at each other with desire darkening their eyes and tension mounting around them.

'Then why in God's name do you behave as though you'd be glad to get away?'

She longed to answer him truthfully, to tell him that she knew about Elaine, but her hands were tied by professional honour. And she knew that it wasn't the past that tormented her, but the present, and the dread that he might still be Elaine's lover.

'I think you have a distorted view of things,' she commented. 'Your attitude these past weeks in particular has cut through so much. There hasn't been any frankness, and your behaviour over Elaine . . .'

'We are not talking of Elaine,' he rapped out fiercely. 'But since you mention her, what about Douglas?'

Andrea exclaimed with all the violence of love, anger and desire, '*You* know all there is to know about Douglas!'

Garth lowered his gaze.

Why wouldn't he tell her the truth? Why the secrecy? Why come here at all if he was not prepared to be honest with her? Of what use words, when shadows lay upon them like cobwebs in an attic?

She said, her voice shaken, her eyes meeting his with fierce accusation, 'I don't trust you, Garth. In so many ways you've become a stranger.'

He stared at her, a dark pain in his eyes, as with a strangled cry he echoed her words, getting to his feet as though unable to endure the inactivity.

'Don't *trust* me?' he repeated, looking down at her accusingly. 'Then there is nothing more I wish to say in any case. I shall never intrude in your personal life again.' His eyes seemed to reach her heart in their deep searching. 'Since you do not wish to dissolve our partnership, I suggest we behave and work together in a civilised manner, like thousands of ex-lovers manage to do.'

She got up with a little cry. Suddenly, violently, he lowered his lips to hers in a fierce passionate kiss.

'Never fear I shall do that again,' he assured her, as he went from the room, and the flat.

CHAPTER SEVEN

THE real time scanner showed that Elaine's cyst was benign, and as a result she seemed impervious to any discomfort and insisted on continuing to work until Friday midday before admission to the nursing home on the Sunday. A silence seemed to have settled upon Clee View from Andrea's point of view, almost as though she had been excommunicated. Garth looked through her rather than at her, his voice and manner merely polite. There was no point at which she could possibly re-open the discussion, or qualify anything that had been said. Had she uttered those words, '*I don't trust you, Garth*'? In reverse, how would she have felt? At every turn she seemed to say the wrong thing, goaded by love and the frustration born of ignorance. It was like holding the muddled pieces of a jigsaw puzzle without having the picture.

There had been nothing but misunderstanding between them since the night she had refused his dinner invitation. Everything had built up then, with Elaine's confidences making progress impossible. And no matter how many times she went over it all, she came back to the same solution: The severance of their partnership, which she hadn't the courage to face. The cliché, that nothing stood still, reinforced the hope that something might happen to change the pattern, so that he would take her into his confidence. As against that, there was Douglas, and the future. She owed him a decision, and knew that the wisest thing she could possibly do would be to marry him—not as a convenience, but as a means of avoiding becoming the love-sick female clinging to an illusion.

Garth sent a message to her through Mrs Boyer, asking if she would look in to see him after morning surgery and before she went on her rounds. They hadn't met as usual that morning to summarise the day's work because he'd been called out to a midder.

When she went into his room, Garth was standing by his desk. He seemed both menacing and challenging, but his eyes searched hers as if making an assessment.

'Sit down,' he said quietly, and as she did so, moved to his chair and faced her across his desk.

'It's about next week,' he began.

She looked blank.

He prompted, a little testily, 'Elaine will be in the nursing home.'

Andrea felt weak and boneless, as though all strength had gone from her spine and only her heart was working in an empty body.

'Of course.'

'I'd like you to see her in,' he said firmly, his expression inscrutable. 'I'd also like you to be on call every other evening while she is in the nursing home so that I'm free to visit her. The few friends she has are either abroad or too involved to make long journeys, and since she won't be ill, the time will seem doubly long.'

Andrea said unemotionally, 'I understand. I shall, of course, be visiting her.'

'Thank you.'

The possessiveness of his tone snapped a little of Andrea's control. 'I *am* her doctor!'

'Of course . . . Courtesy comes into it,' he said archly.

And all the time they were watching each other. Was

he remembering? Emotion seemed to be a living force between them which no politeness, no pact, could destroy.

He said, like a man clinging to the purely professional stabiliser, 'I lost Mr Vaughan this morning. Massive coronary.'

There was a second's silence; her voice was low, 'I'm so sorry. I know he was eighty and had enjoyed a good life, but . . .' She paused. 'I understood you were at a midder—Mrs Borthwick.'

'True; the baby came first.'

'Now *I* must go to see Mrs Ranleigh. By the way, there was no heart involvement. Hiatus hernia.'

'You'd an idea that it was,' he said, remembering. 'Can't beat you as a diagnostician.'

They were on familiar ground; two people bound together by a profession they loved and to which they gave all their concentration and concern.

'It's *proving* a thing,' she said.

They looked at each other and almost immediately away again. Comment could so easily have led to argument.

Andrea got to her feet. They nodded, and she left. Once outside the door she stood, trying to regain control, to return to some semblance of normality.

Clare came upon her unexpectedly, and gasped, 'Dr Forbes, you look so pale.'

Andrea managed a laugh. 'Must have forgotten the blusher this morning!'

Clare glanced at Garth's door as though it would yield up a secret. If you asked her, there was something very strange going on between Dr Howard and Dr Forbes. So polite; so distant. And there was Nurse Drake purring all over the place, like a well-fed tabby—despite the prospect of her operation. It certainly wasn't only in doctors' surgeries that the weird things happened! It was in their private lives, she reflected.

When Andrea told Elaine that she would see her into the nursing home that Sunday, she exclaimed, 'Was that Garth's suggestion, may I ask?' Her voice was honeyed, her expression faintly smiling.

Andrea didn't prevaricate. 'Yes.'

'You'd think no one had ever had an operation before,' came the amused remark. 'And it's so simple. Oh, don't get me wrong; I'll love having you with me, but it seems a bit of an imposition.'

'Not at all. I know them all at Merrifields.'

'It would have looked a little odd if Garth had accompanied me,' Elaine suggested confidentially. 'His visiting me will be different. You won't stop people gossiping, anyway,' She looked down in a moment of silence, before saying in a low voice, 'There's a question I've been wanting to ask you—as a patient. How long after the operation before one can make love again?'

Andrea felt that her temperature had gone up to 105°. The words were uttered so naturally and with such obvious implications.

'As a nurse, I'm sure you know it's around four weeks.' Andrea's emotions churned, making her voice unsteady. How dare Garth be so affronted when she said she didn't trust him? Why should she? She wanted to add, 'And it is a ridiculous question, since Garth is a doctor and it would be discussed anyway.'

'I just wanted to be sure. These things have to be taken into account, and discussing them makes it all so *medical*. Hardly romantic,' she added, knowingly. Then, looking at Andrea very levelly, she hurried on, 'By the way, Dr Jayson spoke to me this morning and suggested that, when all this was over, the four of us should have dinner together at a rather special restaurant he knows. I was most surprised.'

'The four of us.' It didn't sound like Douglas, and yet there was absolutely no point in Elaine distorting the truth. And why should Douglas telephone her, anyway?

Andrea asked Douglas that question when she had dinner with him at the Crooked Inn near Clun that evening.

'I always like to reassure my patients,' he said easily. 'And the getting together was a spur-of-the-moment thing. It is obvious that she is pretty well entrenched in Garth's life. You must realise that.'

Andrea tensed. She said too casually, 'Oh, I do.'

'I only felt it when I spoke to him the other night: his attitude . . . Time he got married—like me,' he finished ungrammatically, holding her gaze. 'Andrea, do we have to wait until we can go out for a day? Can't you make up your mind *now*?'

Andrea felt that life was whirling around her; that all her preconceived notions about it had been shattered, leaving only disillusionment and suffering. She was tired of hanging on Garth's every word, analysing his behaviour; hurt and bewildered by his relationship with Elaine. Wasn't it time she struck out for her own happiness, and future? She loved Douglas more than enough to marry him, and probably her feelings for Garth could be likened to the teething troubles of romance and sexual awakening.

In a breath she said, 'Yes. Yes, Douglas. I don't need any more time.'

'You mean you will *marry* me?'

She nodded and put her hand out across the table to meet his.

She never forgot that moment in the old inn, with its massive log fire roaring and lantern lamps glowing. She had sealed her future, and there was a deep affection in her eyes as she looked at Douglas admiringly and with gratitude because he seemed to have saved her from herself. Loyalty would demand that, from now on, she saw Garth only as a professional partner, even as he had stipulated. She must forget his words, *'Never fear I shall do that again.'* In any case, she thought with annoyance, what kind of a man was he who'd kiss her at all when Elaine was in his life? He was, in fact, betraying them both.

Douglas studied her intently, his love for her deep and unselfish.

'I want to make you happy,' he said solemnly.

'You will,' she promised. 'I shall leave Clee View . . . have a year's freedom.'

'Are you serious?' He sounded amazed.

'Quite . . . Devote myself to you—how's that?'

'Wonderful! Perhaps ultimately to join me? Take over the midder side.' He watched her as he continued, 'Garth will be lost without you.'

'The truism that "no one is indispensable",' she retorted. 'He won't be surprised about *us*!'

'No,' Douglas agreed. 'He's pretty perceptive, but there's a part of him I cannot quite fathom. It's as though he retreats into a private world—like a man with a secret.' He added deliberately, 'I've never admitted that before, or been able to give it expression.

She said chidingly, 'I didn't get engaged to discuss Garth!'

'True.' He changed the subject. 'I hardly know your mother—what will she say?'

'She is not involved with my life,' Andrea sighed.

'We've very little in common. I suppose it could be said that I neglect her because I rarely go to Tenbury Wells. I telephone; but it is never *right*. No welcome; always a grumble. She wanted to live with me after my father died, and I knew that wouldn't work. She was still a young woman and refused to make a life for herself. Now she complains of being lonely. You cannot change a disposition, unfortunately. If I went to see her every night, it would be wrong because I didn't go in the afternoon, also.'

'Life's strange,' he said ruefully. 'My mother believes that freedom is the greatest gift you can give to any child, next to love. She and my father went to America, where he had business interests, and finally settled in California. My sister Natalie has been there with them since the spring, and is thinking of making it her permanent home. She will never be a problem so far as we are concerned.'

Andrea nodded, and said a little later, 'We'll have to go to Tenbury . . . Obviously, I'll ring Mother tomorrow.'

When finally they left the Crooked Inn, the mists were rising over the fields. The harvest moon had waned, but the sky was light and cloud-rifted; the smell of autumn pungent and smoky. Shropshire lay like a vast garden, dignified and magnificent with its rolling meadowland and distant Welsh hills. No one was about as they reached the car on the car park, and Douglas drew her into his arms, saying, 'I've been longing to kiss you, and I don't care who might see us!'

Andrea closed her eyes and clung to him as if seeking salvation.

'I love you, Andrea.' The words were uttered softly as his eyes looked down into hers in the blue darkness.

Her answer was to raise her lips to his in a great yearning to be able to repeat those words with the same depth of meaning. She thought, even in that brief moment, that there were many facets of love, and once she was Douglas's wife, everything would have a new dimension, and the bond between them bring a fulfilment she had never before known. The vital thing was not to look back, but forward. The silence around them seemed to reinforce her resolve, bringing a curious peace, and confidently she slipped her hand into his as they moved the few paces to the car doors and he saw her into her seat. Andrea felt that she had changed her entire personality in those moments, as she clicked her seat-belt into place. They looked back at the old inn; its lighted windows seemed like smiling eyes gazing benevolently upon them.

Andrea didn't see Garth until the evening of the following day, Friday, since their schedule was thrown out of gear through Andrea beginning the morning with a call to a seventeen-year-old youth, Tommy Knight. He had swallowed a murderous cocktail of tranquillisers for kicks at the flat of his girl-friend, who was in such a state of shock that she too had to be taken to hospital. He was put on a respirator, remaining in a coma. Andrea was left to deal with the respective parents, who were devastated not only by the events, but by the mode of the life generally, having been accustomed to 'respectability'. From that tragedy, she rushed to a self-induced abortion which, by a miracle, escaped the dire consequences, the mother's life being saved by prompt and skilled hospital treatment. As a bonus she delivered a much-wanted first child—a girl—of a happily married couple who had waited five years to conceive. After surgery that evening she flopped at her desk, hoping that a little of the mental stress would vanish. Now her thoughts concentrated on the fact that she must tell Garth about her engagement. And while she had no illusions that it would mean anything to him, nevertheless it was bound up with finality, from her point of view.

He appeared in the doorway, startling her, and seeing him standing there swirled her memory back to the spring evening when he returned from his holiday. She shut out the memory with a sharp admonition. Nostalgia was a disloyalty to Douglas.

'I hear you've had quite a day.' He spoke almost as though he were giving a reason for being there.

'Tommy Knight,' she said. 'You know the Knights . . . I thought he and his girl-friend were two reasonable people, according to modern standards. They both are in well-paying jobs . . . Now, what have we? He could remain in a coma, his girl-friend is frenzied, and the parents of both of them are too stunned for it to sink in. If I had my way, I'd hang drug-pushers of any kind. Belligerent? That's how I feel at the moment. How can I *help*? If he remains in a coma, do you switch off the machine?' She stopped and looked apologetic. Where work was concerned, she and Garth were in complete accord.

'I understand exactly how you feel. Come and have a sherry. Relax for a few minutes before you go home.' It was the partner speaking.

They walked together to his sitting room.

Drink in hand, she took a deep breath and came face to face with reality. This was the ideal moment to tell him about Douglas. The complications were merely in her own vivid imagination. She didn't want to notice Garth as a man, as distinct from her partner, or to remember every line of his fine body and its nearness to her own, or to recall the ecstasy before sleeping in his arms. It suddenly seemed ludicrous that she was going to marry Douglas, and she panicked at her own decision. She struggled to sustain the atmosphere of calm professional sympathy that existed between them at that moment.

Their eyes met as they raised their respective glasses.

'I'm going to marry Douglas,' she said, lowering her gaze and then managing to look at him very levelly.

There was a moment of electric silence; the stillness between them unnerving. He made no exclamation or gesture of surprise, and his acceptance made her wince, as he said, 'I wish you every happiness, and congratulate Douglas. I'll ring him.'

Her heart was thumping as she sat there, tortured by the fact that he had not trusted her with the truth; that behind the magnetism lay the flaw of deception. Emotion warred against emotion: the love she genuinely felt for Douglas, the need of his support and peace of mind, against the torture of being *in* love, with all the passion and desire, the fury and even hate, embodied in the words.

And suddenly, startlingly and with vehement emotion, he said, 'There's one thing I must tell you, Andrea . . . When I came to see you at the flat, I had important things I wanted you to know. It didn't work out that way, and now there is no earthly reason why they should concern you. The right decision so often rests on a knife-edge of wisdom. And when it comes to it, we are not very wise where our emotions are concerned.' He changed his tone abruptly. 'And now to practicalities.' He implied that he had no intention of enlarging on anything he had said. 'Are you planning to marry soon?'

'Things I wanted you to know.'

Andrea felt slightly sick. There was so much to be read into that; so much conjecture. Obviously it was about Elaine . . . Her own words, *'I don't trust you'*, seemed to be written in flame, searing her. But she could not plead for his confidence, having just told him she was now going to marry Douglas. And she knew that Garth was expecting an answer to his question, defying her to avoid it by asking another. If only she didn't have to sit there, hands tied, unable to break a confidence. If only she could ask him if he and Elaine were still lovers. But she said quietly, 'Reasonably soon; obviously not before Christmas.'

'And announce it?'

'Next week. I shall tell them here, and now that you know . . .' She caught at her breath, feeling tension and emotion rising between them in an inescapable wave. 'There will be a lot to arrange,' she rushed on disjointedly. 'I want a year without working.'

'A good idea! I shall have to look for another partner,' he said solemnly and got up from his chair, pouring himself another drink with a gesture of resignation.

Subtly, insidiously, their mood had changed. Her engagement had thrown the past into relief, not eradicated it. She thought of his last kiss, and his words which now seemed haunting.

'You will have plenty to choose from.'

There was a stern implacability about him in that moment.

'I shall get a locum to begin with. Male,' he added firmly.

A shutter might have come down between them.

'Elaine is going to stay at the Feathers when she leaves Merrifields.' It was like a note of dismissal, so far as their previous conversation was concerned. 'It was arranged only this morning, so you won't have heard.'

'I thought her daily was going to take over for a week or so?'

'She had to go to Shrewsbury. Her mother is ill.'

'Probably be better, anyway.' Andrea was watching him closely; his brow was furrowed.

'Yes,' he agreed. 'I was never keen on the other arrangement, but Elaine can be very stubborn. Doesn't take advice gladly.'

Andrea gave him a look which, interpreted, suggested, 'You should know,' but she merely remarked, 'It is always tedious to be restricted when one isn't ill, and it is merely a matter of convalescence.' A shiver went over her as she recalled Elaine's question about making love . . . Was that one of the 'important things' he had wanted to tell her?

'I shall be glad when all this is over,' he said a trifle impatiently, thinking of Elaine and how, despite his efforts to the contrary, he had become so involved.

Andrea stiffened. 'Elaine will almost be home this time next week,' she retorted.

'I . . .' He stopped, not wanting the matter discussed.

'Douglas and I are going to Tenbury to see my mother, after I've taken Elaine to Merrifields on Sunday . . . Will you take the calls?'

'Of course.'

It flashed through Andrea's mind that at least a hotel would be impersonal when it came to Garth visiting Elaine after she left the nursing home.

The telephone rang, and they gave each other an enquiring look. But it was Elaine.

Andrea went to the door and said quietly. 'Good

night, Garth. You can tell Elaine about Douglas and me.'

Garth did so, and at the other end of the line Elaine sat with a look of sheer delight and satisfaction on her face. Everything she had plotted and planned for was being achieved. The engagement was the final triumph, but she was not deceived by it. Andrea was not in love with Douglas, but with Garth; and that had constituted a menace. Now, no matter what Garth's feelings might be, Andrea was out of reach.

'They're ideally suited,' she purred. 'But poor you.'

'What do you mean?' The question was sharp.

'Having to find another partner,' she hastened, mindful of his tone of voice.

'I shall have a locum to begin with.'

'I came in at the right time,' she said softly.

He couldn't deny that, or her usefulness in the practice. 'True.'

'You sound tired,' she said sympathetically, and added, 'Do you know if the wedding is to be soon?'

'Reasonably so, I believe.' He didn't want to discuss Douglas and Andrea. The wound was raw.

Elaine said tactfully, 'I won't keep you talking . . . Good night, Garth and thank you for helping me to decide about the Feathers. You're absolutely right, of course.' Her voice was full of conviction.

Garth replaced the receiver and stood looking down at the instrument. Again he found himself reflecting that one couldn't fault Elaine these days . . . and, just in that second, he was almost grateful for the diversion she provided. He didn't want to reflect on Andrea's engagement, or his own feelings. He disliked muddle and secrecy, and seemed doomed to be a part of both. At least the problem of Andrea had been solved, cancelling further conjecture. For all that, it would have been very easy for him to convince himself that the former passionate attraction they had experienced still lingered. A dangerous concept when all his loyalty was centred in his friendship with Douglas.

Elaine's operation passed off without complications; she ran a slight temperature afterwards, but progressed normally otherwise. Andrea saw her from time to time, aware that Garth visited her regularly, seeming obviously relieved when, eventually, she returned home and took up her duties at Clee View again. She had genuinely been missed, and her arrival that first morning brought a sincere chorus of welcome.

'I can't believe I'm really back,' she said, beaming at Mrs Boyer, Clare and Andrea as they gathered in Mrs Boyer's office during those first moments. 'I don't think I've been a particularly good patient, but at least I could understand the nurses' point of view . . . Dr Howard not in?'

'A pneumonia; old Mrs Green. He'll get her into hospital, I expect.'

Elaine nodded. 'When I saw him last night, he expected to be here to greet me,' she said easily. 'Now I'd better glance through the list and try to click back into routine. Thank you for the flowers: I've been thoroughly spoilt! Ah, that's Garth now.' She hurried into the main hall, where he was shedding his coat. The weather was bitter, with an icy north-east wind to herald the beginning of November.

Andrea did not miss the meaning glances exchanged by Mrs Boyer and Clare.

'I reckon we shall have another engagement before very long,' Clare said. 'Nothing like a little operation to speed things up, and no one can say that he hasn't been attentive!'

'No one should say anything,' Mrs Boyer admonished. Then, turning to Andrea, 'You've your friend Mrs Barnes this morning, Dr Forbes. Last on the surgery list.'

Andrea remembered the appointment. Harriet, twenty-five, was a vital extrovert who'd had trouble in finding the right pill. She always enjoyed Harriet Barnes's company. This was probably to say she was pregnant. There was a boy of two, and they wanted another child.

Garth and Elaine stood in the doorway of his consulting room as Andrea reached it on the way to her own.

'Just one moment before we start.' Garth nodded to Elaine as she walked away with an air of self-satisfaction. 'Come in, Andrea.'

'Douglas spoke to me yesterday,' he said, walking towards his desk. 'He's very anxious that, now Elaine is fit again, we should have the dinner already talked about. It is a question of arranging it with you. Elaine will fit in with whatever is finalised. I believe you've found a place near Aston on Clun.'

'Yes. I'm sure you and Elaine will like it. We thought, seeing it is November at the weekend, that it might be a good idea to make it Sunday lunch.'

'Splendid.' It did not escape his notice how easily she associated him with Elaine, realising, almost with a pang, that it was inevitable and inescapable.

'Then shall we make it this Sunday? Brian will stand in.'

'Very well. We'd better go in two cars,' he added cautiously.

'Yes, you and Elaine can follow us. Meet at Douglas's house, about eleven-fifteen?'

'Very well.'

She fingered her solitaire engagement ring and his eyes followed the gesture, then looked directly at her—almost, it seemed, in challenge.

'If it's foggy . . . well, there are plenty of alternatives on our doorstep,' she hastened.

'Some early November days can be very beautiful.' The words were stilted, the atmosphere tense.

Unconsciously, she sighed. 'I wish we were walking towards the spring instead of the winter.' She felt that she was coming out of a trance as she exclaimed, 'And *I* must be walking to tackle surgery.'

Again their gaze met. Neither spoke as she left.

Harriet Barnes came into Andrea's room without her usual elasticity of step or smiling face. There was a hunted look about her, and fear in her eyes. Depression seeped from her like a mist, and her voice held a note of doom.

'My dear Harriet!' Andrea said, alarmed. 'Whatever's the matter?'

'Everything,' came the flat reply. 'And now that I'm here . . . nothing seems real any more. I can't believe that one's life can change completely overnight. It's all so terrible—so horrible.'

Andrea cried, 'What is terrible—horrible? Harriet! What has happened?'

'You'll despise me, and I don't expect any sympathy or understanding, but I've got to tell someone or I'll go mad . . . mad!'

'Doctors are here to try to prevent that,' Andrea said gently. 'There's *nothing* that can't be dealt with. Tell me.'

There was a moment of heavy, almost unbearable, silence as Harriet drew on her courage, and then words rushed out, almost wildly, agonisingly. 'Alan was away for the night, Mother looked after Tim, and I went to a party . . .' Harriet's face was so pale that Andrea thought she was going to faint, her normally bright eyes were wide and subconsciously appealing. 'I . . . I had too much to drink and let a perfect stranger make love to me. I didn't really know what I was doing, or if I'd even recognise the man again!' She covered her face with her hands, great dry sobs racking her body.

Andrea went to her emergency cupboard and poured out a small brandy. 'Drink this.' Her words were sympathetic, but authoritative. How many times, she asked herself sadly, had she heard a similar confession? But its familiarity in no way minimised the tragedy.

Harriet drank gratefully.

'And now,' Andrea prompted encouragingly and with quiet gravity.

'And now I'm pregnant!' came the horrific whisper. 'Alan and I wanted another child, as you know, and I haven't been on the pill for six months . . . Don't you see?' She looked at Andrea like someone pleading for a miracle.

'Yes.' Andrea suppressed a sigh. 'There's no way you can tell who the father is?'

'No. It happened immediately after my period.' She added with disgust, 'The man was just a charming stranger.' She shook her head. 'I despise myself as much as you must despise me. I must have been mad!'

Andrea said swiftly, 'I'm just so sorry!'

'It wasn't *like* me. I've never thought of another man. I love Alan, and we're so wonderfully happy . . .' She went on disjointedly, 'Champagne always makes me foolish—reckless, if you like. I remember being out in the garden. It was a beautiful night . . . He kissed me, and everything after that was like a fantasy. Oh, how can I expect anyone to understand, or wish to do so?'

Andrea's sigh was deep and full of feeling. 'It is my job to understand, and even if it weren't, I'd want to.'

Harriet relaxed slightly. 'When I realised what had happened, the shock sobered me a little. I excused myself from the party and didn't see him again. I drove a little way and sat in the car until I was in a fit state to face my mother. Millicent Wain, who gave the party, is a great friend of mine, and apart from the usual eulogies and light-hearted gossip afterwards, nothing was said. She wasn't even aware that I had left early, and if she was, she would have thought it was because of Timmy.'

'And Alan knows you're pregnant?'

'Yes. We live far too intimately for me to have missed two periods without his noticing. He's thrilled, and has put my depression down to pregnancy symptoms . . . I've tried to tell him. Each day I say to myself, "This evening, I will." Smash everything he values; his faith in me, his marriage, the utter *misery* . . .'

Andrea said solemnly, but almost briskly, 'So you've decided to salve your own conscience at his expense, and by wrecking his life, yours, and Timmy's?'

Harriet started, her eyes opening wider as she said in a breath, 'What do you mean? I can't live a lie—palm another man's child off as his own! I'm not quite such a monster.' A curt note crept into her voice.

'And you don't think you'd be a monster if you took a hammer and smashed his life?' Andrea added, 'No one in this world could possibly say that the child is not his. So that would be another life you'd ruin.'

There was an electrical silence.

'You—You mean I should have a—a miscarriage—a convenient termination?'

'That is the last thing,' Andrea told her. 'No, I'm suggesting that *you* face the hell, *you* do the suffering and learn to live with your conscience in order to spare Alan.'

'Oh, no!' She looked appalled by the suggestion.

'If you cannot face that,' Andrea said briskly, 'you'll have something far worse on your conscience—the destruction of a family.' She fixed Harriet with a steady gaze. 'As I see it, if this had been some clandestine affair with all the deception that goes with it, that would have been a different matter. But wreckage of this kind in order that you may feel virtuous at having done the right thing—No! You can't weigh a possible fifty years of marriage and family life against a moment of too much champagne and folly with a stranger. That folly is your debt, and you should be the one to pay it. I don't underestimate the hell your silence will bring, or what it will cost you. But that is the price.'

Harriet looked stunned. 'I've never lied, or pretended, to Alan . . . As you know, we were childhood sweethearts.' Now the tears rolled down her cheeks, and she burst out, almost in a frenzy, 'I know: If that is so, how could I have done what I did? That's what people would say, and they'd be right.'

Andrea said gravely, 'I'm only interested in your marriage and Alan, and what will be your *children*. I beg you to think of them before you take any steps. And because you have missed two periods,' she said, almost as an afterthought, 'it doesn't necessarily follow that you are pregnant.'

'I've been sick, my breasts are tender . . . I *know*.

Alan knows . . .' The words were a whisper. 'He'd —He'd probably forgive me . . .'

'And bear the burden of your guilt, surrounded by shadows? Don't condemn him to live that way if the child should not happen to look like him. Oh, Harriet, there is so much at stake!'

Harriet sat very still. In imagination watching Alan's face, should she tell him the truth; feeling the sickness she would suffer were it he who had been unfaithful? The word sounded ridiculous, almost obscene. She didn't remember anything but a whirl of excitement and then the sudden shock of realisation as she'd run away . . . If only she could wipe it out. 'Dear God, help me,' she whispered. 'Give me the courage to bear it; to accept the trust in Alan's eyes . . .'

'My dear,' Andrea said gently, 'if I've sounded brutal and dogmatic, forgive me. But I've seen a little of all this, and it can, at this stage, never be more than the lesser of evils.'

'I know you're right,' came the quiet acceptance. 'Unburdening oneself is a luxury I cannot afford.'

'And no sackcloth and ashes—outwardly,' Andrea warned. '*Their* right is happiness; and without your contribution, that wouldn't be possible.'

'Happiness!' Harriet shuddered. Then, 'If I hadn't been able to tell *you*, I think I'd have . . .' She stopped, and rose to her feet. 'I'll come to see you professionally next week. Alan takes that for granted.'

'I'll look in for a drink from time to time, also,' Andrea promised. 'But all this must never be mentioned again. You owe Alan that, too. Self-pity is not an ally of courage.' Her expression might have implied, 'And you'll need every scrap of that.'

Andrea told Garth the story, without mentioning

Harriet by name, later on that day. They were alone in the common room for a few minutes, and he listened, standing with one elbow resting on the filing cabinet as he drank a cup of coffee.

'Do you agree with me?' she asked finally. 'Is it . . .' She stopped, sighed, and gave him a vulnerable look that stirred powerful and inescapable emotion. He put his cup down on a near-by table.

'Is the lie of silence justified if it saves the wreckage of a family?'

His answer surprised, even shocked, her with its passionate undertones. 'I'd prefer the silence—anything rather than lose the woman I love.'

Andrea was comforted by his reassurance, but shattered by his words, '. . . *anything rather than lose the woman I love.*'

It was in the present tense, and could only mean Elaine . . .

CHAPTER EIGHT

SUNDAY arrived, clear and bright. Frost lay over the fields, glistening like snow while the trees still held a tint of autumn, tenacious leaves remaining bronze and gold as if smudged by a painter's brush. They reached Aston on Clun via Stokesay, with its castle (once, in the thirteenth century, a fortified manor house) etched against a cloudless blue sky. Aston itself was noted for its huge oak, which, by a tradition going back over two hundred years, was draped with flags of all nations every Royal Oak Day, the 29th May. Two round stone houses completed a picture which gave the village a distinction as well as charm, the story being told that they were built in that shape to avoid corners in which the devil might hide.

The peace of Sunday hushed the land in an atmosphere of worship, with church bells echoing in a paean of praise while, later, the ringing of tills in the old inns betokened merriment—Aston's Kangaroo Inn having, perhaps, the most original name.

The Barn restaurant was off the Clun road—tucked away as though it were a secret known only to connoisseurs of good food. It had been converted from an old coaching inn built around 1745, and was a splendid example of Queen Anne style.

'This only goes to show,' Garth said, as he and Elaine joined Douglas and Andrea, and they stood beside their respective cars on the car park, 'that there are always places to discover where least expected.'

'With Clun Forest on your doorstep,' Douglas added.

Elaine looked delighted. 'It is all new territory to me,' she said appreciatively.

Inside, there was the comfortable atmosphere of a country house, its dining room attractive with pink and beige carpet, and watercolours on the walls. One of several large windows looked out over a spacious garden, at the bottom of which children could be seen riding their ponies.

Douglas had reserved a special corner table, and the champagne was already on ice.

'This is just a mini-engagement celebration,' he said when they were settled in their chairs, having had an aperitif in the lounge. He studied Elaine closely, and she felt unnerved by his scrutiny. He did not deceive himself —this meal was not wholly for the purpose he had just outlined. Elaine had roused his curiosity, and knowing her during the past weeks had deepened his conviction that he had met her before; also, that there was something about her which didn't ring true. Garth's involvement sharpened his interest. And it had not escaped his notice that Andrea was too guarded in her assessment of Elaine. Thus he was left with an uneasy feeling of doubt and suspicion foreign to him. He was quick to notice Elaine's proprietary attitude towards Garth, subtly manifested in ways of which its subject appeared to be totally ignorant.

The table d'hôte luncheon—the best choice on a Sunday—was, among several options, roast turkey, and they all selected it.

Elaine enthused, 'It is awfully kind of you, Douglas, to include me in this outing. I always have loved going to new places.'

'You're settled in Ludlow?' Douglas said, looking at her intently.

'Oh, yes! I can't imagine ever wanting to leave it.' She flashed Garth a meaning smile, and then looked at Andrea, 'Unless they should not want me at Clee View any longer.'

There was a second's silence, which Douglas broke by insisting, 'I'm sure you would be greatly missed.'

'As has been proved these past weeks,' Garth said.

The champagne was served.

Andrea sat there feeling isolated, avoiding Garth's eyes, yet drawn to him by some magnetic force; aware that he was there with Elaine, thus throwing into relief Elaine's confidences, making her own body throb with emotion and rejection. The situation seemed ludicrous, and she clung to her relationship with Douglas as a means of fortification. He was the reality; the future. Living in the past was not only foolish, but futile. Nevertheless her gaze met Garth's immediately after he had proposed a toast. For an instant, passion flamed between them, and then a shutter came down as he returned his glass to the table.

She faced with dismay a generous portion of turkey with all the trimmings, and the vegetables on a side plate. If only she could have sat there and sipped the champagne, instead of trying to force food into an unwilling stomach which, while feeling empty, was nauseated by the prospect of food. She felt, rather than saw, Elaine's gaze upon her, and drew on her courage, taking a deep breath and turning to Douglas as though for salvation.

But he was sitting transfixed, studying a watercolour within easy range of their table.

'What is it that fascinates you about that picture?' she asked.

Silence had descended: suspense crept upon them like a ghost appearing at dusk.

'The artist's name,' he said with a clipped decisiveness. 'Gordon Tate.'

'Means nothing to me, I'm afraid,' Andrea said frankly. 'Which no doubt proves my ignorance.'

Garth's expression was wary, and Elaine drew in her breath audibly.

'Now,' Douglas said easily, 'I know where I've met you before, Elaine! I told you I never forget a face.'

She simulated a blank expression. 'I'm completely in the dark.'

'I met you at a party given by Jerry and Trish Roxburn. Hyde Park Square, about five years ago.'

She laughed outright. 'And what has that to do with Gordon Tate? As for remembering me at a party five or so years ago . . .'

'Gordon Tate was at the party. He was well known in art circles.'

Andrea did not miss the enquiring, somewhat suspicious, look Garth cast in Elaine's direction as she gave a little hollow laugh. 'My dear Douglas, I've never met Gordon Tate in my life. If I had, I'm hardly likely to forget the name, because his success would have been a topic of conversation. Like Andrea, I must admit to never having heard of him. Neither do I know a Jerry and Trish Roxburn. I must have a double.'

'I talked to you,' Douglas said, memory stimulated by concentration. 'There was a young doctor chap there, a Christopher somebody . . .'

Elaine broke in, 'You are definitely confusing me with

someone else! I've never been to Hyde Park Square, and haven't even any idea where it is.'

'Near Marble Arch—off the Bayswater Road.'

Andrea was drawn to the whiteness of Elaine's knuckles as she increased her grip on her knife and fork. She seemed anxious to make her point, as she added, 'I still shouldn't be likely to forget a party where a well-known artist was a guest, even if I had been ignorant of his name to begin with!' She smiled; a smile that seemed to be painted on her lips. 'I'm sorry I can't help you.'

Both Douglas and Andrea noticed the frown that furrowed Garth's forehead and narrowed his eyes, and he spoke with the faint impatience of one who wished the conversation to end.

'I marvel that anyone remembers anyone at parties, let alone their names! Half the time the noise deafens you, and you couldn't care less to whom you are talking. And after five *years*!'

'I shouldn't forget that particular party,' Douglas assured him. 'The edges may get blurred, but . . .'

'Then you must, as I've said, put my double among the blurred edges.' Elaine insisted on what she hoped might be a note of humour, as she darted a quick look at Garth, who was still unsmiling.

'I will,' Douglas promised, but Elaine was left with the uncomfortable feeling that she had not convinced him and that he was merely being courteous in not pressing the matter further. 'Ah, well,' he continued pleasantly, 'it has jogged my memory, and I must try to get in touch with the Roxburns again. We've mutual friends. Now, what's next on the menu?'

'Just coffee for me, please.' Elaine looked subdued.

They were all in agreement, but conversation flagged

and there were uneasy silences. Garth was normally an excellent and witty guest who could be guaranteed to choose interesting topics, but there was a mask-like grimness about him which no amount of feigned cheerfulness could conceal. Sipping his coffee, he suddenly said, looking from Douglas to Andrea, 'Have you fixed the date for your wedding?'

Somehow it was the last thing Andrea expected him to ask.

'*I've* suggested next week,' Douglas said with a wry smile.

'Forgetting that I have professional commitments,' Andrea retorted indulgently, nerving herself to look at Garth.

'I'm not making any major decisions,' Garth confirmed. 'I've already said that I shall get a locum, so you need have no qualms on my account.'

It wasn't what Andrea wanted to hear. The thought of leaving him and Clee View tore at her heart, but she said, trying to keep a note of defiance from her voice, 'I think we might say March, don't you?' She turned to Douglas as she spoke. 'The beginning of spring.'

Douglas looked delighted. 'Can I have it in writing?'

'With pleasure! At the church!'

Garth said, 'Seeing this is the beginning of November, that gives me a breathing space of nearly five months. Say four, because you'll want some respite, and probably leave me in February.'

His words hung between them with an increasing tension; neither looked at the other.

Douglas, startled, sensed the atmosphere. Was Garth secretly unsympathetic towards Andrea's decision to leave him—quite apart from the obvious fact that he would miss her as a colleague?

Elaine spoke up in a rather admonishing tone. 'You're being very phlegmatic, Garth.'

'That is your interpretation,' he said, rather brusquely. 'Andrea and I have a perfect, professional understanding.'

Jealousy flamed, which Elaine could not contain. 'Why the qualification?'

The innuendo was not lost on Douglas, neither was the dark anger behind Elaine's smile. She had not convinced him about the party, and he had no intention of letting the matter rest there. She was obviously manoeuvring her way permanently into Garth's life, and thus, as a friend, he had justification for seeking to confirm his suspicions, nebulous though they might be.

When they had finished their coffee and returned to their respective cars, Douglas said, 'Shall we go back via Leintwardine, or . . .' He paused, 'We could then . . .'

Garth spoke quietly but firmly. 'You and Andrea go off on your own now. I'll see Elaine home, and I've some correspondence I must catch up on . . . It's been a splendid lunch, and this is a delightful place.'

'Delightful,' Elaine echoed.

And they each knew that the outing had not been a success; that it had resembled an egg without salt.

Once in the car, alone with Elaine, Garth said, 'Why did you lie about that party? About not knowing Gordon Tate, and . . .'

She reddened as she said, trying to keep calm, 'I didn't *know* Gordon Tate!'

'You'd met him; met him with Christopher, because he told me. It's no good, Elaine, I'm tired of this deception. There's no reason for it, and I want the truth to be known.'

'You wouldn't!' she cried. 'The past is . . .'

'Up to a point, a secret that only you and I share, but that's only one facet. For the rest, I want them to know of our relationship, and if you don't tell them, I shall. For God's sake, how long do you think it can be kept a secret? Many people know, and, as you've seen today, Douglas wasn't fooled. I know he wasn't. Far better to have said openly that you'd been there, and the matter would have ended.' He cast her a sideways glance, 'Incidentally, have you seen Gordon Tate recently?'

'No,' she said rather harshly. 'I believe he went to live in the south of France. And I never did know the Roxburns very well, anyway.'

'But you didn't have to deny Christopher. I hated every second of it!'

She said pathetically, 'Oh, Garth, don't drag up the past—not like that. Let things stay as they are. When Douglas and Andrea are married, we can tell them.'

'Whatever has their being married got to do with it?'

'Just that . . . Oh, I don't know,' she said, looking distressed. 'I suppose I ought not to have come back into your life, but what I told you was so true, and we've become friends. Don't let's spoil it all. Nobody is being hurt. Our past is our own, after all.'

That was true enough, Garth thought dismally, knowing that everything had got out of hand because of his silence and the circumstances prompting it.

Elaine believed, or deluded herself, that if nothing more was said about Gordon Tate and Christopher, the subject would be closed. 'At least,' she said after a brief silence, 'you know where you are so far as Andrea leaving the practice is concerned, but you can't operate permanently with a locum.'

'I shall try to find the right man,' he retorted with finality.

'Come to think of it, you are surrounded by women.' Her laughter was false. 'Four, to be exact.'

He frowned. It offended him for Andrea to be classed as one of a number.

Elaine kept the conversation inconsequential for the rest of the journey, and when they reached Broad Street, Garth said on a note of weary depression, 'Let's stop at Clee View. Edwards and Lily are working today from choice, and will get us tea a little later.' He had a desire to be in his own home rather than to be invited into Elaine's, should he take her back. Correspondence had been a lame excuse to escape from any possibility of another foursome that evening.

Elaine felt the suggestion was in the nature of a triumph, and that the earlier disharmony had been wiped out. A short while later, when they were settled in the sitting room, she mentally planned the changes she would make when she was mistress of the house, as she fully intended to be. It was a question of playing her cards carefully until March, when Douglas and Andrea were married. She felt the stab of jealousy because there was no doubt in her mind that Garth was in love with Andrea, and she with him. She knew, also, that her confession, about her and Garth being lovers, had been a major factor in their emotional disharmony. Andrea would never break that confidence. Elaine congratulated herself on having manoeuvred the whole situation with skill. Her own love for Garth had built up to a passionate fervour, and with it had come a tenacity and determination to overcome any obstacles, no matter what deceptive part she might be called upon to play. It was ironical that her trump card was the integrity of the two people whose happiness she was intent upon destroying. Garth appeared to be blind to the assumptions that were being made about his own affairs, and unaware how closely her name had become associated with his. He was like a man living in a detached world, observing life from afar.

The ringing of the telephone, after they had had tea and were thinking in terms of a drink, brought forth a little groan from him.

'I'll answer it,' Elaine said at once. 'Nurse Drake can assess, and possibly save you having to go out!' She lifted the receiver. Then, '*Andrea!*' Her voice dropped.

Andrea thought, even in that second of emergency, of Garth's excuse about catching up on correspondence.

Garth reached the telephone and had taken the receiver from Elaine's hand before she could say any more.

'Anything I can do for you?' He spoke pleasantly.

'Yes,' she said urgently. 'The Gresham baby—Toby. I think it's meningitis, but I need your opinion.'

'Where are you speaking from?'

'The Greshams' house. You know of them—they live near Quality Square. I delivered Toby. Fortunately Douglas and I were at the flat when Mrs Gresham telephoned.'

'I'm on my way,' he said.

Elaine was sitting firmly in her chair. Garth had picked her up that morning, so she was without a car.

'I can drop you,' he said swiftly, as he put the receiver down. 'You get your coat.'

'I can easily wait,' she suggested as he strode towards the door.

'Better do as I say. One never knows with these cases.' He hurried to have a word with Edwards, who was excellent at taking any messages that might come through. 'I'll keep in touch,' he said as he flung open the front door for Elaine to precede him.

Elaine fumed. She had been looking forward to a cosy evening when she and Garth might have struck a more intimate note. She knew, however, that she had dropped out of his world and that as he had told her about the case, only the sick child exercised his thoughts.

Andrea saw Garth with an overwhelming relief, murmured a few words to Ronald and Meryl Gresham, and went straight into the blue and white nursery, with its nursery-rhyme wallpaper and cot painted with cuddly animals. A lovable-looking teddy bear sat in a miniature armchair by the bed, as though keeping sentinel. The room had the hush of sickness; the light subdued.

Toby, just a year old, had a high temperature. He was lying curled up on his side in a stuporous condition, and became irritable when disturbed. There was stiffness in his neck and a certain rigidity of his spine. He looked pathetic and terribly vulnerable, his fair curls tumbling over his forehead.

Garth said gravely, 'I'm afraid you're right. We can't wholly complete the diagnosis or determine the cause until we've had a lumbar puncture. Hospital . . . immediately.'

Andrea said, 'There's always such fear with a child.'

'Would you like me to make the arrangements?'

'Would you?' she begged.

'Of course.' They talked as they walked out of the room, the parents waiting apprehensively at the bottom of the stairs.

'Dr Howard will have a word with you when he's done the telephoning. I'm afraid it means hospital,' Andrea said gently.

Garth told them quietly and honestly what the situation was.

Meryl Gresham echoed the word, *meningitis*, with horror, reaching out for her husband's hand as if for protection. 'But that—that can cause brain damage, or—or epilepsy!'

'Now,' Garth said quietly, 'we mustn't bring alarm into this. There are various types, and until we've done a lumbar puncture—drawn off some cerebrospinal fluid—we can't be specific. Speed of treatment is vital . . . Why didn't you send for Dr Forbes earlier?'

Meryl Gresham looked guilty, and at the same time, concerned. 'We didn't want to worry you on a Sunday. Children are so often sick and feverish for no reason, and bouncing about an hour or so afterwards.'

'They are also sick and feverish for many grave reasons. Never again fail to send for us if Toby isn't well.' He spoke deliberately.

Ronald Gresham said half-sadly, half-apologetically, 'Toby came to us when we were old to be parents, and we've not had much to do with children, but he's—he's become our life. Doctor . . . He will be all right?'

'Everything will be done. Now, if you'll get a few things together . . .'

'And go with him,' Meryl Gresham said immediately. She looked at Ronald, trying not to appear too distressed by the fact that he could not accompany her. His mother, of nearly ninety, lived with them, and couldn't be left without arrangements being made.

'I'll help you,' Andrea said, mounting the stairs. At

that moment, Meryl Gresham, flaxen haired, white faced, looked distracted, her dark eyes frightened and appealing.

They put a few tiny garments, beautifully knitted and kept, in a small case. There was something unbearably pathetic about those small personal possessions when related to the silent little figure lying so still in his cot.

'He must have his teddy bear,' his mother said poignantly, not able to take in how desperately ill her son was. Tears were running down her face, although she was not making any sound, or effort to wipe them away, just moving like an automaton programmed to efficiency.

The ambulance came and left. Ronald Gresham stood transfixed in the icy November air, watching, it seemed, his world collapsing around him. The night before, at this time, he and his wife had been sitting in their comfortable home watching television, oblivious of the devastation twenty-four hours could bring.

Garth and Andrea went back into the house with him. Garth looked round for the drinks tray, and unceremoniously poured a brandy. 'You need this,' he said gently.

Ronald Gresham took it gratefully.

'I hate my wife going alone . . . not being with them . . . We haven't told Mother anything. She's rather deaf. Everything *will* be done?' he pleaded disjointedly.

'Everything; and children are very resilient,' Garth reassured him.

It was ten minutes later when he and Andrea left the house. The blind of forgetfulness lifted the moment Andrea faced him by their respective cars, bringing back memories she ached to forget. He had been with Elaine when she telephoned him. She had interrupted their evening *à deux*.

'Thank you for coming,' she said with feeling. 'It was like dealing with dynamite.'

'I'm a doctor.' He hurried on, fearful of being misunderstood, 'I should have been glad of your opinion, I assure you. I wouldn't like to make any prognosis, but pray God the little chap pulls through without any complications.'

Neither wanted to leave; the pull of attraction amounted to pain, followed by overwhelming depression. Emotion gave them immunity from the cold, and their eyes met in the darkness, each struggling to conceal the need that quickened their heart-beats.

'Are you . . .' Garth began, and stopped.

'I'm going to have supper with Douglas at West Close. He went home when I got this call. I'm afraid I interrupted your evening with Elaine.'

He made no comment: a terrible *ennui* lay upon him. He didn't want to go to Elaine's flat; neither did he want to go back to Clee View and spend the evening alone.

'You'll get cold,' he murmured, and opened the driving-seat door of her car.

She took it as a gentle dismissal, and got in.

'You'll be in touch with the hospital?' he suggested.

'Yes. I'll probably go there; depends on his condition.'

'Bad business. If only patients would send for us, instead of deciding——'

Andrea cut in, 'Ironically, it's always the serious cases when we're needed, and the trivial ones that do waste our time. But nothing is ever too trivial with a child.'

His gaze held hers, having grown accustomed to the darkness.

'This has upset you.' He spoke softly.

Her voice was shaky. 'I'm very fond of Toby. They'd given up hope of ever having a child, and were not young. They're a happy couple.'

'I know.' He made the words almost profound. 'Drive carefully,' he said, as he shut the door.

Yearning brought a lump to her throat, and tears stung her eyes. If only the clock could be put back!

She saw him through the driving mirror as she moved away. He stood there, motionless.

During the week that followed, Andrea found herself studying Elaine almost through X-ray eyes, her conversation with Douglas coming sharply into focus. It had been robbed of its importance by the illness of Toby, who was making satisfactory progress, bacterial meningitis having been diagnosed and the condition responding to antibiotics.

'Do you and Douglas want children?' Elaine asked abruptly at the end of the evening surgery and as she was in Andrea's room.

'Yes.'

'Brief, and to the point! Is anything the matter, Andrea? Oh, I know you've been worried about the Gresham boy, but you're not my idea of a happily engaged girl. You should be sparkling!'

Andrea felt that she was being put under the microscope, and resented it. There was something very smug about Elaine these days, as though she had scored some secret triumph and was enjoying every moment of it.

'I don't have to grin like a Cheshire cat to be happy,'

she retorted rather bluntly. 'Garth and I have some very sick patients on our hands and we care about them.'

The 'Garth and I' came like a blow for which Elaine was not prepared, and the fact that it was true and formed a bond between them rubbed salt into the wound, increasing her jealousy.

The intercom went, and Garth said, 'Is Elaine with you?'

'Yes,' Andrea replied.

'Would you ask her to come in. There's something I want to say to her.'

Elaine smiled. 'We haven't decided about dinner tonight,' she said as she hurried towards the door. 'Garth does like everything cut and dried—always has.'

But Garth wanted to see her about a patient's blood pressure. 'I double checked,' he said gravely. 'You had it 160/90, and it was 190/100.' He fixed her with a critical gaze. 'If you are going to . . .'

'I never get the blood pressure wrong,' she cut in. 'There must be some mistake. Must be the effect you have on the woman! She's blood-pressure mad, anyway.' In that minute she let her temper and her jealousy make him the whipping-boy, but she recovered herself almost immediately. 'I'm sorry. Forgive me. I don't usually let my feelings for patients affect me. Of course I must have made a mistake . . . put the wrong figures down on the chart.'

'We can't afford to make mistakes,' he reminded her.

She felt a churning annoyance and could not keep her feelings under control, despite her apologies. 'Do you usually double check my work? If so, my job seems superfluous.'

'This happens to be the first time I've done so. It was because Mrs Peter's symptoms seemed extreme, and her bouts of giddiness distressing. I saw for myself.'

'Could have shot up while she was with you?'

'Possible, but highly improbable . . . Anyway, be doubly careful in future.' He paused, looked at her very directly, and spoke in a firm, almost challenging tone. 'I'm going to get Douglas and Andrea over for a meal one evening next week and tell them the truth about us. Or such truth as is possible to tell. The situation is untenable, and offends me,' he said with a somewhat brutal frankness. 'Your coming back into the picture puts a vastly different complexion on the matter. I've gone along with your wishes so far.'

'You haven't told them, then?'

'Prevarication, and a reluctance to tell half a story,' he confessed.

Immediately she rushed in, 'You will still be telling them only half a story.' A little gleam of triumph flashed into her eyes, but, knowing him, she appreciated that his mind was made up and that she would be foolish to try to dissuade him. On reflection, taking Douglas and Andrea into their confidence might strengthen her own position. But she said with a sweet reasonableness, 'Whatever you wish,' and a certain relief touched her.

'We'll fix an evening,' he said, and spoke to Andrea on the intercom, asking her to join them.

Elaine went over to Garth's desk, standing behind it as he sat down. As Andrea came into the room, she made a gesture giving the impression that she was moving swiftly away from an embrace.

Garth jerked sideways to avoid her arm as she hurriedly took a step towards the window, aware that Andrea could imagine only that an intimate scene had just taken place and that Garth had sat down abruptly at his desk.

The atmosphere, the suspense, brought an awkward silence, before Garth said, 'I've some important matters I want to discuss with you and Douglas, so could you arrange to have an evening here early next week? A buffet meal, perhaps.'

Andrea, faintly alarmed, baffled and a little suspicious, said tentatively, 'Yes, I'm sure Douglas could fit that in.'

'Monday?' There was a degree of urgency in Garth's voice.

'Very well; if possible, Monday. I'll speak to Douglas tonight.' She looked at him, and the words rushed out, 'Is anything wrong?'

Garth replied evasively, 'No, just a matter of setting the record straight.'

Andrea felt that all the blood had drained from her body; her heart thudded. Were he and Elaine going to announce their engagement? There was no question but that she had just witnessed the end of an obvious love scene as she came into the room, the fact giving credence to the possibility. Didn't his words, *'setting the record straight'*, emphasise the likelihood? And, she told herself angrily, what did it matter, since she was going to marry Douglas?

Douglas came to her flat that evening, and the moment she saw him she was aware of an element approaching the dramatic in his manner as he greeted her, poured out their drinks in silence, and then said, 'I've something to tell you that will come as a shock.'

Andrea felt that her skin was lifting from her flesh and that icy water being poured between the layers. The moment of silence seemed like an eternity, as she cried, *'What?'*

'Garth and Elaine . . . She is his ex-wife!'

CHAPTER NINE

ANDREA heard the words, '*She is his ex-wife*', and knew she was going to faint; sliding to the floor as Douglas reached her side.

He knelt beside her for a second, saw that she was lying flat and then hurriedly whipped a clean handkerchief from his pocket, wrung it out in cold water from the kitchen tap, returning swiftly and placing it at the back of Andrea's neck. She was already stirring; white, her skin cold and clammy; immediate awareness of the situation making her struggle to get up.

Douglas continued to hold the handkerchief in place until a few minutes later—his arms supporting her. He helped her the short distance to the sofa, where she lay back against the cushions, feet up.

'I said it would come as a shock,' he exclaimed quietly, and with a cautious and critical eye. 'But not to this extent!'

'I never faint,' she said, and forced a wry smile.

'Then you've just given a good imitation!'

And all the time the words were drumming in Andrea's brain . . . '*ex-wife*'.

'But why,' she said, unaware that she was answering her own question by asking another, 'why the secrecy?'

'That's what interests me. I knew Elaine was lying about Jerry and Trish Roxburn. I've often had an unpleasant feeling that Elaine has some hold on Garth, and that there's compulsion somewhere along the line about their association. The mere fact of being married and divorced is nothing, but their attitude, her working with him—the whole situation is a mystery.'

And as she lay there, Andrea was crying inwardly, Why hadn't he told her? Why, even when they were *together*? And Elaine's insistence that they had been lovers; that they were still. Where did the truth begin and the lies end? Why should a man link up again with his ex-wife unless he loved her?

She asked Douglas abruptly, 'How did you find this out?'

'By ringing an acquaintance with whom I'd lost touch. We both knew the Roxburns, but he'd never met Garth. Apparently Elaine married Garth soon after that party, and they divorced very rapidly. Jerry and Trish are in America at the moment, by the way, or I'd have had a word with them.'

Andrea thought of Garth's invitation for the following Monday, and his reference to having important matters to discuss, 'setting the record straight'. She explained it to Douglas, who said, 'It's possible that he intends telling us then. I suggest we keep quiet,' he added forcefully. 'My own reaction is an inherent distrust of Elaine, and, after all, Garth is my friend.'

Andrea said somewhat belligerently, 'Doctors don't usually employ their ex-wives. As his partner, I see no reason why I can't ask him why he has been so secretive.'

'I'd rather you didn't,' Douglas said firmly. 'There's something very strange about all this. If they don't want to tell us, fair enough. I can't rid myself of the suspicion that, no matter what the circumstances, Elaine isn't to be trusted in any situation.' A thought struck him. 'I suppose it's possible that they have just remarried! Maybe that's what he has to tell us.'

Andrea caught at her breath and struggled to control her emotions. The dread possibility appalled her.

Douglas changed the subject. 'And now,' he said, on a note almost of curtness, 'we've had enough of that. It has upset you too much already.' She looked away, and said hastily, 'We must eat.'

She realised that he was watching her not only with a professional eye, but almost with a suspicious one. The atmosphere had altered: the sudden silence was full of unspoken questions. She got unsteadily to her feet, insisting that she was all right and had only a casserole dish to serve.

'Then I'll get it out of the oven,' he insisted with authority. Then, pausing for a second, said, 'Andrea?' His voice was solemn.

'Yes?' She felt apprehensive.

'You won't alter the March date—will you?'

Almost with defiance and aggression she replied swiftly, 'That is the last thing!' Her devotion to Douglas had never been greater than at that moment. She felt she never wanted to see Garth again. His whole life was a sham and a pretence.

Andrea could not anticipate events as she changed that Monday evening, choosing a pencil-slim ruby velvet dress which subtly revealed her perfect figure. She fingered her engagement ring as though it were not merely a token of love, but a protection. Loyalty to Douglas calmed her as she drove to Clee View with confidence reinforced by determination. Nevertheless, she felt that she was waiting for the curtain to go up on a drama as she saw Garth and Elaine standing together, almost as though receiving her at some formal function.

Elaine said immediately, 'Douglas has just telephoned; he's on his way from Cleobury Mortimer. A pneumonia.'

'Oh!' Cleobury Mortimer was twelve miles away, but it seemed two hundred in that moment.

Elaine added spontaneously, 'What a lovely colour your dress is! There's something so rich about velvet, too.'

The compliment was lost on Andrea. She could see Elaine only as having once been Garth's wife, which explained the unusual relationship. That was emphasised, as Andrea reflected upon it.

Garth looked straight into Andrea's eyes, aware that during the past days her manner towards him had become more reserved; that the chasm between them had widened. 'Sherry?' he enquired.

'I'd prefer a gin and tonic.' Andrea wanted to get away from old habits. She'd had sherry at the flat, and here, with him, alone.

He looked surprised, but served it. 'I hope that will be to your liking.'

'A vodka martini for me, as you know,' Elaine put in.

'Douglas will not mind our being ahead of him,' Garth said as they raised their glasses a few seconds later. He was having his usual whisky.

Were they lovers? Were they remarried? The questions rushed through Andrea's mind despite her efforts to maintain detachment. She fell back on 'shop' as she said, 'The Greshams cannot understand why Toby should have got meningitis. They couldn't appreciate that it can be contracted through close contact with a person carrying the organism, without their having the disease . . . Toby's making steady progress still. But now the mother has 'flu, and at her age . . .'

Elaine said without sympathy, 'She will have to die

some time. *I* don't want to live to be ninety . . . always a responsibility to someone.'

And while Andrea agreed with her in many ways, she countered, 'Wait until you reach the age.' Her voice was sharp.

Elaine's eyes widened; there was something prickly and contrary about Andrea, she thought, and had been for some days.

Douglas arrived and they settled down, but with an underlying uneasiness.

Garth said suddenly, almost abruptly, 'There's something I have to tell you.' He looked first at Andrea, then at Douglas, and back to Andrea.

Andrea's nerve broke; all the passion, the emotion, the lost ecstasy and the yearning came with her words, 'You don't have to bother, Garth. We know that Elaine is your ex-wife.' There was a withering scorn in her voice. 'It has been a well-kept secret. Why, only you know. *Friendship* should involve trust.'

There was a shocked, disbelieving, silence. Douglas called out, sharply admonishing, *'Andrea!'*

Andrea, white, shaken, regained a little of her composure, her voice shaken as she murmured, 'I'm sorry.'

Garth's voice came like the lash of a whip, 'How long have you known?'

Douglas said quietly, 'Since last week.'

Andrea lapsed into silence, heart thudding, a sick sensation of self-criticism washing over her as she realised that her outburst had been ill timed, and had angered Douglas, who had counselled silence.

Elaine flushed; she felt just then that Douglas constituted a menace and, even as Garth had insisted, was fully aware that she had lied about the party. She hated being at a disadvantage.

Garth got to his feet and stood looking down at them from the chimneypiece. Andrea's scorn shrivelled him. He appreciated how contemptuous she must feel about his silence, but his hands were still tied, and an aching sense of loss stole over him.

'This evening was planned so that we could tell you.'

'It is your business,' Douglas said quietly. 'But, as your friends . . . Well . . . In fact, we wondered if you might have remarried.'

'No,' said Garth almost grimly. 'We haven't remarried.' He couldn't fall back on even valid excuses, since he could not give the true story. Whichever way he looked at it, he could not speak out. He felt awkward and ill at ease; Andrea's challenge enfeebled any attempt he might try to make by way of explanation. 'We were married and divorced in just over two years,' he added.

Douglas intervened, 'Let's leave it at that. As friends, we are interested, but not prying. The matter would not have become a subject for conjecture, had it not been for the reference that Sunday to my having met Elaine before.'

Elaine had made only gestures and uttered the odd exclamation, but now she said a trifle defiantly, 'Garth and I were not married until after you *thought* you had met me.' She had no intention of giving ground, despite the fact that Garth was aware of the truth. She sensed danger with Douglas who, if so inclined, could unearth facts she had fought to conceal. She changed her mood to a faintly flippant note. 'Well, now that our guilty secret has been disclosed, could we go into the dining room and have something to eat?' She added, with a trace of mockery, 'If Garth and I remarry, we shall give you due notice. We're flattered by your concern and interest. You both have an unfair advantage: I'm sure neither of *you* has a secret past!'

Garth frowned, but found refuge in silence as they walked to the door and into the dining room where an attractive buffet meal was set out. He was conscious only of Andrea, and the contempt that showed in her eyes as they happened to meet. Her outburst had stripped from him the dignity of explanation, making him seem a traitor even to friendship. He had no weapons with which to fight, and knew that only by clinging to reserve could he hope to survive. He was fair enough to appreciate that, were their circumstances reversed, he would share her contempt and not give any quarter.

The rest of the evening was like treading on eggshells. Only Elaine sailed through it with ease, dismissing the prospect of Douglas being a danger, no matter what he might discover. In any case, he was not the type of man ever to cause trouble. If Andrea had been able to control her emotions, the evening would have gone off smoothly, and, unless she was very mistaken, Douglas would not even have mentioned the fact that he already knew the truth. Andrea had, in short, given her the triumph, emphasising the importance of being the ex-wife.

'I can't think what possessed you to speak out as you did!' Douglas said to Andrea as he was driving her home. 'We'd agreed to say nothing. Far better not to have given any hint that we knew. I was staggered!'

Andrea had no explanation that she could voice. Love, jealousy, disgust—every warring emotion had gone into her outburst, the tone of her voice, the flash of her eyes, revealing an involvement which was the last thing she wished to betray.

She fell back on genuine apology. 'I've no excuse,' she said quietly. 'But I've worked with Garth, thought I knew at least a *little* about him, and all the time . . . I'm sorry, Douglas.' She sighed, and added, 'I wouldn't have annoyed you for the world.'

'We'll forget the whole wretched business. Why on earth there's been all the secrecy, beats me. You notice how glad Elaine was to drop the subject, without any question of how we discovered the truth? And her attitude over that previous meeting . . . Garth's silence was inexplicable, too. I don't want to dwell on it. I value his friendship, and I honestly believe that Elaine would be delighted to ruin it. She intends to remarry him, mark my words.'

Andrea said sombrely, 'I agree with you.'

She faced Elaine at the first opportunity after evening surgery the following day. 'Why, as my patient, did you lie about you and Garth being lovers?' she demanded.

Elaine had a look of indulgence on her face that was condescending. 'Oh, Andrea, don't be so naïve! Because I happened to have been married to him doesn't mean that we'd not been lovers previously, or are not lovers now. You seem to be very interested and involved with Garth's private affairs. If he'd wanted to take you into his confidence, he would have done so long ago. My confiding in you was all part of my being your patient. If you weren't engaged to Douglas, I'd say that you were in love with Garth. Or am *I* being naïve, now, and you *are* in love with him anyway?'

'I'm not talking of my feelings,' Andrea protested, trying to keep her voice steady.

Elaine looked at her long and unnervingly. 'If you ask me, I don't think you *dare*. The story of Garth's life and mine has been rather extraordinary. It is a long one, and we guard it jealously. And since you seem so interested in our affairs, we have deliberately waited before remarrying so that we should not make a mistake for the second time. But love is a strange emotion, as you well know: there are some people who just cannot live without each other, when it comes to it. We were foolish to break up our marriage and ought never to have been divorced in the first place.'

'You remarried,' Andrea pointed out.

'Yes. Not for love, to be frank, but for companionship and financial security. I don't profess to be a noble character . . . But Garth didn't remarry,' she added smugly. 'Oh, there have been other relationships, but they haven't meant anything to him. He's been quite honest.' She gave a little indulgent laugh. 'He was furious at your outburst last evening. After all, there's no reason why he should have told you, or anybody, about his life.'

Andrea was very still. Her world was in ruins in any case, and she smarted under the burden of her own folly, but she had no intention of allowing Elaine to be patronising. Pretence was over; the thin veneer of friendship was peeling under the stress of deception. Her voice was cool and impressive as she said, 'Both as my patient and as a friendly colleague, it's my belief that you have twisted the truth to suit yourself, Elaine. You've had an ulterior motive, and you'd stoop to any mean trick to further your own ends. I may be naïve, but I am not deceived. Your relationship with Garth is your own business, but I don't think you would like me to repeat the stories you have told?'

'I've confided in you as my doctor!' Elaine burst out fearfully and stridently.

'Protected by the privilege of the doctor–patient relationship,' Andrea said sharply. 'You wouldn't have trusted *anyone* otherwise. I am not concerned with what is true, or not true, but don't take me for a fool. You came back here with one object in mind—to get Garth to remarry you. So don't make up any more lies, because I am not impressed!'

'Nevertheless, you will never have the consolation of knowing the truth.' There was a gleam of triumph in Elaine's eyes. 'Poor Andrea, I'm sorry for you. It must be hell to be engaged to one man and madly in love with another. I spoke just now of that being a possibility. That was naïve of me. There is no possibility about it. Douglas isn't getting a very fair bargain, is he?'

Andrea shivered as though in the presence of evil. There was something predatory and cunning about Elaine as she sat there, confident, ready for any attack, because it was a matter of indifference to her what weapons she used.

Elaine's love for Garth was like a fire; an obsession that enabled her to play any part life might dictate. She had not intended to antagonise Andrea, but now that she had done so, she thought with satisfaction, she could easily draw back from the friendship which had served her purpose. Andrea's attitude the previous night had given her a lever with which subtly to alienate her and Garth still further. She stopped there, appalled by the enormity of her own scheming, a feeling of supersitition creeping eerily upon her as she doubted, for a second, her unparalleled luck. She always got her own way in the end, and this time would not be any different, but she must not lose her nerve.

'I doubt if you could even spell the word "fair", let alone appreciate its meaning,' Andrea said, and walked out of the room.

Andrea saw Garth alone later that evening. She had

stayed on to study some reports and catch up on letters that had to be written by hand. She didn't know whether Elaine had left, or where Garth was, only that she was on call.

He appeared in the doorway, about to turn the light off, and then said, surprised, 'You still here? I saw the glow from under the door . . .'

'Catching up on the paperwork,' she said, all strength draining from her, the memory of the previous evening tormenting her.

It was as though they were two people who had fought to the death and were weak and agonised by their wounds.

She said suddenly, but with deep sincerity, 'I'm sorry about last evening.'

His voice was low as he replied, 'You had a valid point. I should have reacted the same had the circumstances been reversed.' He added, 'Sometimes anger is one's only weapon.'

Their eyes met, their gaze falling away, the silence like a pulse throbbing between them. If only, she thought, she could see him without pain, hurt, and longing.

'The things we don't understand,' she said in a breath, 'we suspect.'

His expression was sad. 'There is nothing more I can say to you, Andrea. You are going to marry Douglas, and my life has nothing further to do with you.'

He made the words sound inevitable rather than contemptuous. He had closed the door and left her no justification for reopening it.

'I agree,' she murmured.

Again they looked at each other, emotion just beneath the surface.

'Explanations without solutions create more havoc than silence,' he said, almost harshly.

'And silence allows imagination to run riot,' she retorted. 'But, as you so rightly say, your life has nothing to do with me. I realise it never has had.' The words rushed out and she saw him wince, stiffen, and lower his gaze from hers.

'In the circumstances, there is nothing I can say to counteract the belief. In a matter of months you will be married, and the book will be closed. Let's not discuss it all any further.'

She said challengingly, 'I wasn't aware that we had *ever* discussed anything; your secrecy—' the words tumbled out—'your *secrecy* . . .' She stopped, her voice breaking, and then regaining strength as she said, clinging to cynicism to prevent her losing all control, 'I find it incredible that you should once have warned me not to get involved *socially* with your ex-wife.'

He didn't speak, but turned and went from the room.

The telephone rang, and she answered it somewhat abruptly, then, 'Mrs Frobisher!' Jan Frobisher was twenty-four, married two years, and had lived with Godfrey Frobisher for a year before then. Andrea felt a proprietary interest in her, and liked her both as a patient and a person. She changed her tone as she heard sobbing at the other end of the line, and cried, 'Jan, what is it?'

'I'm going to kill myself . . . I can't go on. *I can't!*'

Andrea said, 'I'll be with you in five minutes. Whatever it is, we can deal with it . . . *Five minutes*,' she promised, and put the receiver down.

There was nothing unusual about the call; would-be suicides were common occurrences, but one couldn't find comfort in the theory that those who talked about suicide seldom committed it.

Andrea found a shaking, tear-stained, demented young girl who looked at her with wild appealing eyes. 'He's left me! Walked out with that scrawny creature, Peggy. For God's sake, we've only been married for two years and I thought we were happy! *Happy!* What kind of a fool does that make me?' She rushed on, 'But I'll show them! If I kill myself, they'll have to face the music . . .'

'You can stop that melodramatic talk at once,' Andrea said sharply. 'I've not come here to listen to your fantasising . . . Sit down!'

'I'm going to be sick!'

Jan rushed from the room, and when she returned to it, white and shaking, she said, 'I'm sorry. I went crazy, alone here . . . We'd talked about having a baby. I was going to stop taking the pill . . . He was stringing me along—fooling me.' She added woefully, 'But, Doctor, I love him! I thought we'd beaten this marriage game.' She looked at Andrea with a sad desperation. 'We didn't go mad, or live it up, and we weren't into drugs or anything . . . Oh, he used to go out for a drink with his pals, and all the time it was *her* . . .' Jan covered her face with her hands and sobbed uncontrollably. 'What am I going to do?'

Suffering struck a chord in Andrea's heart; she felt that she was almost sharing the experience.

'A wife always has the greater advantage. If you want him back, then put up a fight! Oh, not belligerently, but cleverly.'

Andrea's words brought forth a toss of the curly dark hair and an aggressive snort. '"*Want him back*"? I wouldn't touch him with the end of a barge-pole!' There was a moment of heavy silence before she cried, 'I don't mean that . . . Oh, we're all supposed to be tough today,' her sigh was pathetic, 'but, when it comes to it . . .'

'You won't solve anything by trying to deceive yourself,' Andrea said, amazed by the fluency with which she could give advice without taking it herself. 'But don't let me hear any more of that nonsense about killing yourself. Stomach pumps are very uncomfortable, and you'd have me to deal with, I warn you.'

'You've always been super . . . I mean, before we were married and I had that miscarriage . . . You see,' she rambled on, 'I found the note just before I telephoned you . . . It was put through the letter-box.' She handed Andrea a crumpled sheet of paper on which was written, *I can't stick things any more. Am going to Peg. Will be in touch. Sorry. Godfrey.*'

'He never did like the idea of being tied. Perhaps if we hadn't married . . . But I didn't push him. Honestly I didn't. You say, fight . . . Very well, that's what I'll do! I'll stay on here. He says he'll be in touch.' She spoke hurriedly, hope generating courage and determination. 'What's *she* got . . . ? I won't go whining home to my parents. As you know, I've got a good job at the beauty salon. Oh, thank you, *thank* you for making me see sense . . . If it doesn't work, I shall at least have tried.'

Godfrey was, Andrea knew, a very immature personality, and easily swayed, as had been proved, but excellent at his job in computers. Andrea felt that Jan had every chance of winning, once the physical excitement and novelty of Peggy had lost their charm. She looked around the well-furnished sitting room, aware of the comfort and air of modest prosperity.

A few minutes later they walked together to the front

door, and Jan cried, 'The telephone! It might be him.' She fled.

The sum total of human happiness and misery could be condensed into those words, Andrea thought as she left the flat.

It was at the beginning of December that Garth said, meeting Andrea as she came into the house after a series of visits, 'If you have a minute, I'd like to talk about Christmas.'

Andrea managed not to groan, dreading the thought of the festivities, the parties—some delightful, but others boring and a matter of duty.

There was a lull before surgery. Elaine had gone out shopping for an hour, and the house had a silent, empty atmosphere.

'Christmas always seems suddenly to arrive after being talked about for weeks!' Andrea exclaimed. 'What have you in mind?'

They had worked together in a business-like fashion since that evening of eggshells. A book had been closed without the story being read to the end. There was always this patient, or that, to create a topic of conversation at a professional level, otherwise they might have been two people in a station waiting-room, catching the same train, indulging in occasional pleasantries.

He met Andrea's gaze very levelly. 'If we could fix something this end, I shall go to my parents.' He paused. 'Elaine will come with me.'

CHAPTER TEN

A thunderbolt might have dropped at Andrea's side. A sick sensation sent a shudder over her body. *'Elaine will come with me.'*

'This question is,' he went on smoothly, 'what have you and Douglas in mind?'

The muscles of Andrea's throat felt paralysed; her voice was croaky as she managed to say, 'We haven't gone into it. As you know, Natalie has been in California with Douglas's parents since the spring, and is staying on. We can fit in.'

The silence was uneasy. Andrea could not face the shock of Elaine going to Surrey; equally she could not boldly ask him if that fact meant he and Elaine were going to remarry. His manner was quiet, confident, faintly aloof.

'I mean,' she hastened, 'I can hold the fort here. Unless there's an emergency, patients mostly give us a rest at Christmas.' That was better, she thought desperately; now she was on safe ground, for he was watching her, his dark eyes penetrating and intense.

'Then I'll take over New Year,' he said gratefully, 'and you can have an extra holiday.'

She recovered sufficiently to say lightly, 'Fair enough.' It was a phrase she never normally used, and was aware that he looked surprised by the terminology. His presence had never been more impressive, his personality more powerful, than at that moment.

'Thank you,' he murmured and went on, his voice

sympathetic, 'I'm sorry Ronald Gresham's mother died.'

Andrea sighed. 'It would have been sadder had she lived. Pneumonia is the friend of the very aged. Toby, thank goodness, is fine . . . Now I must have a word with Mrs Boyer, or she will be chasing me for the Mansell report.' She walked to the door and looked back at him as he stood beside his desk. 'At least we've got Christmas settled. I shall manage to see my mother sometime during the break. She is not best pleased that I am marrying a doctor.' The words rushed out and gave her courage. 'Mother's aversion to medicine is almost pathological!' With that she left, shutting the door behind her, the ordeal over.

Alone, Garth gave a little groan, put his elbows on the desk and bowed his head in his hands as he murmured hoarsely, 'Oh God, Andrea; if only I could tell you.'

He didn't hear Elaine come into the room, or know that she had caught his muffled words. She gave no indication that she had been aware of them, neither did she allow her jealousy and fierce resentment to betray itself. 'The shops are packed . . . I always say I'll get my Christmas cards in October, but never do,' she said.

Garth got out of his chair and appeared to be studying some correspondence before looking up and meeting her gaze. In that moment she saw the dark agony in his eyes, and knew that he was making a supreme effort to be cheerful, as he remarked, 'Thank heaven I have Mrs Boyer to take most of that off my hands, and Castle Bookshop is excellent.' He straightened himself, envying Elaine her bright mood, thankful that after the episode with Douglas everything had settled down into humdrum routine; and while he could not approve of her deception over the party, there were certain factors to take into account which excused her in some measure. She had been more than usually considerate and studied him professionally at every level. Her idea of accompanying him to his parents for Christmas had taken him by surprise, but since she knew them, and there had not been any animosity at the time of the divorce, they were quite happy to receive her, never having understood the break-up of the marriage in any case.

'You look weary,' she said softly and sympathetically. 'Do you good to get away . . . You haven't had a break this summer.' She studied him closely and said, somewhat startlingly, 'Does my friendship help, Garth?'

He stared at her. 'That's a strangely phrased question.'

'Well, I'm not so insensitive as not to realise that something is worrying you. You're distracted all the time when you're not working. I'd like to think that I could offer a little diversion. That's not quite the right word, but solace sounds sentimental.'

Garth said honestly, 'Now that our relationship is accepted, I value your friendship.' He made the remark almost as a revelation, appreciating that she had carved a niche for herself at Clee View and would be missed, even as had been said before. This, however, seemed different; more personal.

'Our friendship with Christopher will always be a bond,' she said softly, then pulled herself up. Hadn't she been Garth's secret enemy where Andrea was concerned? Responsible, even at that moment, for his suffering? She tossed her head in a little defiant gesture. Such reflections were self-defeating. If her plans worked, she would return from Guildford as his future wife. She wanted to go to him in that moment, slide into his arms, tell him she loved him more than she thought it possible she could ever love any man. She had been such a fool in the past, thrown away gold for dross, but now life had given her another chance.

Garth looked solemn. 'One can never forget . . . Never,' he said.

'Oh, Garth,' she whispered, her voice full of emotion.

He lifted his head in a gesture half of fear, half of astonishment. He was the last man in the world to flatter himself, but something in her manner breathed the word 'love', and he was shocked and dismayed. That was not a complication he wanted. An icy sensation of apprehension washed over him. Was he blundering blindly into disaster by drawing the ties of friendship closer, or was his imagination running riot? He consoled himself that it was the latter, but, cautiously, as though preparing his defence in advance, he said, 'You and I have an understanding that makes friendship simple and doubly valuable.'

Something in his tone filled her with alarm and she echoed, '"Understanding"?' She added swiftly, 'Of anything in particular?'

He looked at her with a frank appreciation. 'Meaning that I don't have to pretend to you, Elaine . . . You *know* I shall never marry again.'

His words were like a death-knell. Garth, she recognised, was not a man to speak idly, and there was a doggedness about him that turned a dagger in her heart. Her voice was shaken, low and deceptively sympathetic, as she said quietly, 'Because you're in love with Andrea?'

He stiffened, but before he had time to offer any rebuke or possible denial, she continued disarmingly, 'I should hardly deserve credit for understanding you if I didn't realise that!'

He relaxed slightly, criticism dying.

Elaine heard the echo of his smothered words, '*Oh God, Andrea; if only I could tell you.*' A little of his torment brushed off on her as she faced inevitable defeat. All her plans, her schemes, ruined by a single statement; a statement that would not be retracted and was not open to manoeuvre. Her hands were clenched; her head throbbing. Yet she had known he was in love with Andrea. Why, then, have been so sure he would marry *her* again? And she knew that her enormous conceit had forsworn all obstacles, ridiculing any possibility of failure. A glimmer of hope pierced the frightening gloom. Even if he never married again, that didn't mean he would be content to live a celibate life. If she couldn't be his wife, she would be his mistress . . . the friend to whom he made love when the mood suited him. Few men could resist that relationship. She took a deep breath. Once Andrea was married, the situation could still change. If she herself could overcome her jealousy and not overstep the mark in any move she made, she could, within the framework of their friendship, come to mean only more to him as time passed.

She said gently, knowing he would not wish for any further discussion, 'Now we must get ready for surgery.'

He looked at her gratefully as she went from the room.

Despite herself, pity stirred within her for the first time. Garth was not the kind of man to love lightly. It would go deep and be permanent. A feeling of power stole over her: she held his, and Andrea's, happiness in her hands. Nothing could take that satisfaction away from her.

Elaine met Andrea walking down the corridor towards the practice quarters, and said brightly, 'At least

I've done some of my Christmas shopping . . . Managed to get a very attractive cashmere cardigan for Garth's mother . . . I expect he's spoken to you about Christmas and told you we are spending it with his parents.'

Andrea's voice was smooth. 'Yes, we've made all the arrangements. By the way, will you take special care over Mrs Petman's TPR (temperature, pulse, respiration)?' Without waiting for any comment, she went into Mrs Boyer's office.

Although it had previously been arranged that Douglas and she should not meet that evening, he called at her flat, and when she saw him standing at the door, gasped, '*You!*'

'Were you expecting someone else?' He spoke banteringly, but his expression was grave.

Andrea flushed. The bell never rang without her thinking of Garth, absurd though it might seem.

'No.' His steady gaze unnerved her.

'The lecture was cancelled; the speaker has 'flu.' He took off his short coat and put it on the hall chair, following her through into the sitting room. 'I have eaten.'

'So have I.'

He moved naturally to the drinks tray, picked up the brandy decanter and received her nod as he poured out two small measures, putting her glass down on a table by her chair and settling himself opposite her. There was anticipation in the air as he studied her intently.

'I want to talk, Andrea. You're not happy—Why? Oh, you've put up a wonderful show, done all the right things and been the ideal fiancée, but I'm not deceived.'

Andrea paled. She could not pretend, or challenge the honest enquiring look that made Douglas such a sympathetic figure. Yet what was the alternative? She said in a breath, 'I'm more concerned with your happiness.'

'Exactly,' he said quietly. 'At the expense of your own.'

'That's not true!' she insisted. 'I promised to marry you because I wanted to do so.'

'But not because you were in love with me,' he said with a devastating frankness.

She looked down at her engagement ring, and a weary unhappiness settled upon her. Douglas was an oasis, and she had drawn on his strength in order to counteract her own weakness, seeking desperately to give him all the affection and consideration of which she was capable in the circumstances.

'It's all right, Andrea,' he said softly. 'I know. I know you love Garth. I just tried to deceive myself, that's all.'

She lowered her head for a second in a gesture of humble admission and then, meeting his gaze, said, 'I believed I could make you happy; that time would solve the problem. My love for you is a deep respect, admiration, friendship. I didn't allow for your perception.' She gave a little shudder, and tears glistened in her eyes. 'Now I've done what I vowed I would never do—Hurt you and made you unhappy.'

'Only because I had to know. Hurt *myself* would be more to the point.'

'Oh, Douglas,' she murmured. 'I'm so sorry; so terribly sorry.'

Emotion tore at him as he asked, 'Does—Does Garth know how you feel?'

She spread her hands in a gesture of negation. 'No! Oh, no! He is far too involved with Elaine . . . They are going to his parents for Christmas.' As she spoke, she took off her engagement ring and added, 'I didn't mean to deceive you. My intentions and hopes were valid, and I'm so sorry I was such a poor actress.'

Douglas cried, 'Please put the ring back.'

'But . . .'

'Don't you see? It is doubt and suspicion that kill, not the truth. Now I can think of all the possibilities, not the unhappiness and disadvantages. I love you, and we can build on that and the fact that I *matter* to you. I'd never let you go unless it was for your happiness. The chapter is closed. I'll have my bad moments and you will have yours, but time can work miracles.'

He crossed to her chair, put his arms round her shoulders and lifting her left hand, kissed the ring as he put it back on her finger. She rested her head on his shoulder, finding sanctuary.

Christmas and New Year passed uneventfully. Snow fell deeply at the beginning of January, enhancing the beauty of Broad Street with its cobbled verges, levelling them and throwing into relief the Butter Cross with its fine stone portico and cupola. Andrea, dressed in a red and white hooded coat which framed her face, gave a little shiver as she met Garth on her way out after surgery. As she opened the front door, a near-blizzard blew in, and the town lights were dimmed stars in the white-curtained darkness.

'You can't drive in this,' he said anxiously, pushing hard against the door to close it as the wind howled round them.

'Black ice won't be any easier to walk on,' Andrea said. 'I love it, but it makes getting about a devil.'

At that moment, Douglas rang, and Garth handed over his personal cordless telephone to her, moving into the sitting room to give her privacy.

Douglas said, 'You can't drive home in this!'

Andrea forced a laugh. 'So Garth has just told me. But I don't intend to walk home.'

'I'll come round and we'll work something out.'

'Douglas! We're *doctors*, not jelly babies,' she admonished.

'A jelly baby would be frozen stiff in this, and I want to have a word with Garth about a patient, anyway. Tell him, will you?'

'And, of course, you are driving?'

'Of course.'

'Chauvinist!'

'Concerned, darling.'

Dear Douglas, Andrea thought as she pushed the short aerial back into place, went into the sitting room and handed the slim, curved instrument to Garth and told him what had been said.

'Ah,' he replied quietly, 'I, also, want to see Douglas. In fact, since Elaine is here too, the four of us can have a chat. I was going to arrange for us to meet because I've something I want to discuss.'

'Discuss?' The word sounded ominous.

He said with faint cynicism, 'Nothing about which you can forestall me this time, Andrea.' He added swiftly, 'My apologies; yesterday is dead.'

They avoided each other's gaze, but there was still that underlying tension and awareness. They had not discussed the holidays beyond the mere polite enquiry as to whether they'd had a good time. Nothing personal, or any exchange of their activities. Elaine, Andrea thought, had seemed subdued, and her manner was less acid and patronising. She came into the room at that moment.

'You're not going out in this!' she gasped, as she saw the way Andrea was dressed.

Andrea slid back her white fur-lined hood and took off the coat. 'I've had orders to stay here. Douglas is coming round.'

Garth rang the bell, and when Edwards came in, he said, 'We'll be three extra. If it is going to inconvenience Lily, I'm sure we'd all be happy with bacon and eggs, or whatever's going.'

Edwards smiled. 'Lily has already said there'd be guests tonight. She's always prepared.'

'Yes, I know. Thank you, Edwards.'

'All we need is a midder!' Douglas said, as he came in a little later. 'It's hell out there—just like a skating-rink, but thank heaven one almost has the roads to oneself.'

The wind howled and whistled round the house. The central heating was up to 25°C, so they didn't notice the freezing temperatures. But all the time Andrea was watching Garth . . . his words, *'something I want to discuss'*, beating in her brain; fear making her tremble.

His expression was solemn, even though his voice was pleasant. He had an air of resolve about him as, having poured out their small drinks—to be on the right side of the law in any emergencies—he remained standing, looking down at them from beside the William and Mary tallboy. 'I've waited until the holidays were over and we were back to normality, before telling you my future plans,' he said.

Elaine spoke first. *'Plans?'*

'I've decided to leave Ludlow, and wanted you all to know, so that there shouldn't be any misunderstanding.'

Andrea froze. Her hands clenched in her lap, the nails digging into her flesh. 'You mean transfer the *practice*?' she said, shocked.

'Yes. You will soon be leaving, and——' he turned to Elaine—'you can stay on if you wish. Nothing is finalised.'

Elaine cut in, her face like parchment, 'But what are you going to do? Where are you going?'

Garth didn't hesitate as he replied forcefully, 'To have a break, to begin with. Then, possibly, to join an old colleague in his consultant practice in Harley Street.'

Andrea asked, devastated, 'But—why?'

'Personal reasons.'

Elaine gave a little whimper so that all eyes were turned upon her as she exclaimed in a tense whisper, 'I know why! God help me, I know why; and I'm responsible.' She knew in that moment that the battle was lost and there were no more wars to be fought. There was no question of her ever being permanently established in Garth's life. The holiday and his friendly impersonal attitude had convinced even her of that. The ice that had been packed around her heart during the past months melted; the anger, bitterness and jealousy died in a wave of self-criticism and disgust as she burst out, 'I'm responsible, and now I can't stand it any longer. I can't stand by and see you destroy everything you've built up here.'

Garth said sharply, 'Leave it, Elaine.'

It was as though she shed a vicious skin in that moment and breathed clean fresh air for the first time for years.

Douglas said, 'You *were* at that party! Why lie?'

'Because it had become a habit,' she replied. 'I've lived a lie for years.' She looked at Garth, and said, 'It began before Christopher died.'

Garth silenced her as he said, 'If Christopher Grant's name is going to be brought into this, then I am going to be the one to tell Douglas and Andrea about him.' He stood there, defying anyone to interrupt, or thwart, him. 'Christopher was a friend, a colleague; we were at school together. He saved my life, and in the process lost his own. But for his courage and bravery, I should not be standing here now. We were involved in a motor accident; he dragged me to safety and . . . was burnt to death as the car exploded.'

Elaine sat still, her face a mask for a second, and then full of pain as she said, 'And you'll never know, unless I tell you, how dearly you have paid for his sacrifice.'

There was a chilling, almost eerie, silence as Garth said, as though in an interrogation, 'What do you mean?'

'That you married me, believing I was to have his child; believing that it was the least you could do to protect his memory.'

'I don't want that discussed,' Garth said with authority.

Andrea felt that she had been put in a vice; every nerve in her body being thrashed, her heart physically hurting.

The silence was only for a matter of an instant, but it was like a pulse throbbing in the room.

'You'll never be free of me, free to tell the truth, unless I tell it first,' Elaine murmured, her voice harsh. 'You see, Christopher and I were never lovers; it was not *his* child. I turned to you because I knew you believed that to be so. You trusted me when I told you I was pregnant by him. You married me without getting anything in return. I *used* you, Garth.'

Garth gave a sharp, horrified cry, 'My God! To think of the torment I went through so that you and the child should be protected.' He shook his head, 'And it wasn't even *born* . . .'

Elaine's lips parted momentarily before she said, 'No,

nature gave a last ironic twist when I miscarried after we were married. I say "married".' She looked at Andrea very directly and with a touch of the old defiance. 'Nothing I ever told you was true; not only were Garth and I never lovers; we never even consummated the marriage. I wanted my freedom as soon as it was possible to get a divorce, but we separated in less than a year. It was an amicable affair, but I always felt that Garth still saw me as Christopher's fiancée.'

'And the man?' Garth demanded, his voice accusing. 'The man for whom you betrayed Christopher?' Contempt blazed in his eyes.

Elaine looked at Douglas for a fraction of a second before saying, 'The man was Gordon Tate. And he didn't want any complications. I thought, like a fool, that he would leave his wife and marry me. When he knew I was pregnant, he found it convenient to move to the south of France. A really hackneyed story . . . That was why I lied about the party. I didn't want any enquiries. Someone always knows. And Garth appreciated only that we were acquaintances . . . So you see I'm a pretty rotten character.'

Garth's control snapped as he cried, 'Why in hell's name did you come back? Come *here*?'

'A whim . . . And I knew you would always be considerate because of the association with Christopher.'

A look of utter disgust spread over Garth's pale face.

'Also,' Elaine went on, 'I'd remarried, as I told Andrea, for companionship and security, and thought it would be rather amusing to work for an ex-husband who had never been a husband at all.'

'Have you ever studied anyone but yourself?' Garth asked witheringly.

'Until now, no,' she admitted, her voice strong. 'But,

you see I fell in love with you and realised what a fool I'd been all along. I've done everything to involve you: been prepared to play any part in your life, stoop to any level, to get you to remarry me. Now I've lost everything I've been fighting for.'

'But what has all this to do with Garth leaving Ludlow?' Douglas asked her.

Andrea had sat stupified, speechless; emotion raging; the agony of knowing how she had misjudged Garth, a torment. The things she had said burned in her memory . . . He could never have told this story and was at the mercy of Elaine's lies. She had always had the guarantee that he would never betray the truth about their marriage. She waited as suspense built up, so that Elaine's answer became vital.

Garth said immediately, 'Let's not go into that.'

For a second Andrea knew fear. What else was there to divulge?

'Oh yes, Garth,' Elaine said with a touch of defiance. 'This time we must have the whole truth. I've done my part.' She looked at Andrea and said quietly, 'He's leaving because he's in love with *you*, and you're going to marry Douglas. I've undermined your relationship with Garth from the moment I came here. I knew you were the one person who could wreck my plans.'

Andrea felt that the room was spinning; every emotion rushed up at her. She dared not look at Garth, who was standing speechless, jaw clenched. The hush in the room synchronised with the abating of the storm.

It was Douglas who said belligerently, 'Perhaps even you may have the decency to leave it at that, Elaine.' His bitterness, anger, and the confirmation of what he already feared, stunned him.

Garth didn't speak for a few seconds, then, looking at

Elaine with withering scorn, exclaimed, 'I might have forgiven what you've done to me, but I could never forgive you for what you did to Christopher! He loved and trusted you, and you betrayed him.' He added with deep emotion, 'He was a fine man.' Then he spoke with a cold contempt, 'All I ask is that I'm spared ever seeing you again.'

Elaine got to her feet; her strength was not built on courage, but on the lies and deceits that had, thus far, protected her in life. It was the ultimate irony that her love for Garth had, in the end, destroyed her. Defeat was like gall, and she felt a wave of resentment towards Douglas sweep over her. He had undermined her security. The old venom was mingled with her new-found compassion. She went from the room without a backward glance.

Garth sat down because his legs refused further to support him. The silence was so deep that the world might have died.

Douglas looked from face to face. 'I think we've all had enough for one evening,' he said quietly. 'I suggest I take you home, Andrea.' He was in command in that moment; still the engaged man.

Andrea agreed without protest. She dared not look at Garth, and she dared not dwell on what Elaine had said about his feelings, afraid that if she once met his gaze she would betray her own, which, at the moment, would seem a treachery to Douglas.

Garth managed to say, 'I think that is the best thing.' He saw them to the door, out into that white, glistening, silent world. He didn't look at Andrea, nor she at him.

Andrea got through the following day almost without being aware of it, reacting automatically to the patients' needs and answering Mrs Boyer's question about Nurse Drake to the best of her ability.

'But she didn't give us any hint that she wouldn't be coming in as usual!'

'Been a bit subdued since Christmas,' Clare said. 'But nothing's seemed quite normal recently, anyway. I've come to the conclusion that everyone who works in a practice needs to see a head-shrinker—sorry, Mrs Boyer, *a psychiatrist*—occasionally . . . Dr Howard looks positively ga-ga this morning. Not with it . . . Probably something to do with our dear nurse.'

'That's enough, Clare,' Mrs Boyer silenced her.

Andrea avoided Garth until after lunch, when she went into his consulting room. And while her heart was racing, her manner appeared to be calm as she said, 'Could you come to see me this evening? At the flat about seven?'

He lowered his gaze and then met hers directly as he said, 'Look, Andrea. Isn't it better to leave things as they are? We had the truth last night, and no good purpose would be served by my enlarging upon it . . . You are my friend's fiancée, and there's nothing more to be said. I'm only sorry you had to be subjected to it all.'

She ignored all that and said, 'Will you still come to see me?'

'But . . .' He dreaded being alone with her, every nerve in his body strained to breaking point; love, desire, anguish flooding over him, demanding every scrap of control.

'There are one or two things I have to say,' she pointed out.

'Oh.' His sigh was despondent. 'Very well . . . Douglas will know.'

'Yes. I've just had lunch with him.'

'Seven, then.'

It struck him that she was very cool and confident. Elaine's words might never have been uttered. Even her attitude was different. More relaxed . . . Yet why shouldn't it be? Her life was secure and happy. In a matter of weeks, she would be married . . .

When the bell rang on the stroke of seven, Andrea went to the door with a confidence that set her heart racing and her pulse throbbing.

'I've had the calls transferred,' he said in greeting, feeling acutely nervous; he could not hide behind evasion or subterfuge. She knew he was in love with her, and that left him defenceless and doubly vulnerable. He could not fathom what she could possibly want to say to him that couldn't have been said at Clee View. Perhaps she felt that she had been unduly harsh in her assessment during the past months, and wished to apologise.

'Is it snowing?' Was it possible that she could appear so normal, so calm, when her whole world was centred on this moment?

'No, but it's freezing, and I skidded on my way here. Broad Street is almost impassable.' He looked round him and couldn't resist a familiar remark, 'This is a lovely little flat.' He did not dare to look at her as he spoke. It didn't matter that she knew how he felt; she was engaged to Douglas, therefore his control was not only vital, but a matter of integrity.

She indicated the drinks tray.

'Will you?' She paused. 'And sherry for me, please.'

He looked at her over his shoulder; their gaze met for a second and then fell apart.

Settled in their respective familiar chairs, she began, 'Garth, I had to see you here quietly, to apologise for so many things in the past; for misjudgments. I feel I ought to have known you better; that being a friend and a colleague . . .'

He interrupted, 'No woman on earth could have reacted other than as you did. If I'd only known, or guessed.' He added bitterly, 'I can imagine Elaine telling you that we had been lovers and still were! Dear God! I almost marvel that you could be civil to me.'

Andrea sat there, aware of him to the point of desperate longing. 'I wasn't very civil the night you were going to tell us that she was your ex-wife . . . I see now why you didn't tell me, but I'm puzzled as to why, when you couldn't do so in the beginning, you nevertheless had chosen to do so on that night.'

Garth was subdued; his inscrutability the more attractive. He was at a disadvantage from every point of view, and dealing with his friend's future wife debarred him from further emotional statements.

'I had given my word in the beginning that I wouldn't mention our farce of a marriage—Obviously, in any case, I could never have explained the reason for it.'

Andrea said gently, 'You must have cared very deeply for Christopher Grant. May I say that I admire you for your loyalty, and can see the picture so very clearly.'

'Thank you.' He concentrated on his drink, avoiding her eyes. 'Reverting to that night . . . It was just that I refused to go on with the deception. I felt such a hypocrite and resented being placed in an invidious position. I'm horrified, as I've already made clear, at the thought of what your opinion of me must have been. Now I can see that Elaine didn't want anything to associate her with the past, in case Tate's name came into it. Douglas proved her to be right on that point.'

The tension was mounting like some powerful inescapable force between them, and he said hoarsely, his manner withdrawn, 'But I'm not here to talk about myself . . . You wanted to see me.'

'The idea of your going away.' She willed him to meet her gaze. The room was hushed; only the ticking of the grandfather clock broke the silence.

'I think that the matter is better not discussed,' he said stiffly, struggling to sound calm. 'You have your life; leave me to mine.' His voice hardened in an effort not to sound dramatic. She looked so desirable as she sat there, her hair shining beneath the lights, her large dark eyes lustrous and inviting. A woman, he thought, desperately, loving and loved. Nothing in that moment could deaden his jealousy of Douglas, or take away the barrenness of his own future. He burst out involuntarily, 'Life's very strange! You were the woman who didn't want any emotional involvement, and now . . .'

'Now,' she told him, 'there's nothing I want more.'

He demanded, 'Do you have to be so brutally frank? I don't need reminding that you are going to marry Douglas.' He rose as he spoke, pale, grim, dogged. 'There is nothing more to be said between us.'

She stood, too, and faced him. 'Ah,' she said softly, her eyes adoring. 'That is where you're so wrong!' She paused for a second, then, 'I've a question to ask you.'

Something in her attitude made him cry, 'For God's sake, Andrea, don't torture me! It's hell enough being here with you like this . . .'

She put her hand on his arm, and looking at him with a passionate earnestness said in a whisper, 'Will you marry me?'

He stared at her, stunned into disbelief. '*Marry* you? You're engaged to Douglas!'

'Not any more,' she told him, holding out her ringless left hand. 'We settled that today . . . Don't you see?'

'"See", without daring to believe.' He was looking down at her rather like a man coming out of a trance, afraid that everything around him would disintegrate. 'You *love* me?' His gaze was deep and passionate.

'I've loved you almost from the beginning,' she admitted. 'Loved you until it hurt.'

'Oh, my darling,' he murmured as he took her in his arms, his lips crushing hers with an intensity that sent a quivering ecstasy over her, his body pressed close to hers, memories swirling back to the hours they had lain together in all the rapture of desire fulfilled. And in that seemingly endless kiss they experienced a rapture greater than they had ever known.

Breathless, they drew back.

'Didn't you ever guess?' she asked him, her eyes looking deeply into his.

'Never.' His hold on her tightened. 'But, just sometimes, I felt that—that . . .'

'I wanted you,' she prompted, and caught at her breath. 'I never ceased to do so, even when I hated you because I loved you so much!' She paused. 'You haven't answered my question. Do I have to plead with a man before he'll agree to marry me?'

His lips touched hers. 'Special licence, my darling. No waiting.'

'And I can stay on as your partner?' There was a lilt in her voice.

'I'll promote you!'

'Say it, Garth,' she whispered, almost shyly.

'I love you, my dearest,' he murmured, as swift desire surged over them.

Their eyes met and then their lips, in an ecstasy of happiness.

The night was theirs . . .

From the author of Gypsy comes a spellbinding romance.

Unresistingly drawn into Rand's arms, Merlyn then had to suffer his rejection, as he retreated into his own private torment where he still grieved the loss of his beautiful and talented wife, Suzie.

How would Merlyn then persuade him that she would be right to play Suzie in a film based on the actress's life?

It took an unseen hand to make Rand aware of Merlyn's own special kind of magic.

ANOTHER BESTSELLER FROM CAROLE MORTIMER

W♦RLDWIDE

AVAILABLE IN NOVEMBER PRICE £2.50
Available from Boots, Martins, John Menzies, WH Smiths, Woolworth's, and other paperback stockists.

TAKE 4 DOCTOR NURSE ROMANCES

AND THRILL TO THE HEARTACHE AND DRAMA OF HOSPITAL LIFE.

THEY ARE YOURS **FREE!**

Reaching the end of a wonderful romantic story is always a little sad – even if it has a happy ending. So why not continue your reading pleasure with four marvellous Doctor Nurse stories – they're yours for the asking, absolutely free. It's our special offer to introduce you to Mills & Boon Reader Service. Thousands of regular romance readers use our subscription service. When you see the benefits you can enjoy as a subscriber we think you'd want to join them. See overleaf for details of our exciting FREE offer...

Mills & Boon

▶▶▶

As a regular subscriber you'll enjoy

★ **SIX OF OUR NEWEST ROMANCES** – every month reserved at the printers and delivered direct to your door by Mills & Boon.

★ **NO COMMITMENT** – you are under no obligation and may cancel your subscription at any time.

★ **FREE POSTAGE AND PACKING** – unlike many other book clubs we pay all the extras.

★ **FREE REGULAR NEWSLETTER** – packed with exciting competitions, horoscopes, recipes and handicrafts... plus information on top Mills & Boon authors.

★ **SPECIAL OFFERS** – specially selected books and offers, exclusively for Mills & Boon subscribers.

★ **HELPFUL, FRIENDLY SERVICE** – from the ladies at Mills & Boon. You can call us any time on 01- 684 2141.

With personal service like this, and wonderful stories like the one you've just read, is it really any wonder that Mills & Boon is the most popular publisher of romantic fiction in the world?

This attractive white canvas tote bag, emblazoned with the Mills & Boon rose, is yours absolutely FREE!

Just fill in the coupon today and post to:
MILLS & BOON READER SERVICE, FREEPOST,
PO BOX 236, CROYDON, SURREY CR9 9EL.

FREE BOOKS CERTIFICATE

**To: Mills & Boon Reader Service, FREEPOST,
PO Box 236, Croydon, Surrey. CR9 9EL**

Please send me, free and without obligation, four specially selected Doctor Nurse Romances together with my free canvas Tote Bag – and reserve a Reader Service Subscription for me. If I decide to subscribe I shall receive six new Doctor Nurse Romances every two months for £6.60 post and packing free. If I decide not to subscribe, I shall write to you within 10 days. The free books and tote bag are mine to keep in any case. I understand that I may cancel or suspend my subscription at any time simply by writing to you. I am over 18 years of age. Please write in BLOCK CAPITALS

Name _____

Address _____

_____ Postcode _____

Signature _____

Please don't forget to include your postcode.

SEND NO MONEY NOW – TAKE NO RISKS

*Mills & Boon Ltd. reserve the right to exercise discretion in granting membership.
Offer expires March 31st 1987 and is limited to one per household. You may be
mailed with other offers as a result of this application.
Offer applies in UK and Eire only. Overseas please send for details.*

EP30D